The Inner Planets Trilogy, Vol. Two

PRIME SQUARED

M. S. Murdock

Cover Art by
JERRY BINGHAM

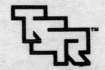

PRIME SQUARED

First Printing: October 1990
Printed in the United States of America
Library of Congress Catalog Card Number: 89-51881

9 8 7 6 5 4 3 2 1

ISBN: 0-88083-863-3

TSR, Inc.
P.O. Box 756
Lake Geneva, WI
53147
U.S.A.

TSR UK Ltd.
120 Church End,
Cherry Hinton
Cambridge CB1 3LB
United Kingdom

Many thanks to all those friends whose support has made the future possible.

The Inner Planets

Earth

A twisted wreckage despoiled by interplanetary looters, Earth is a declining civilization. Its people are divided and trapped in urban sprawls and mutant-infested reservations.

Luna

An iron-willed confederation of isolationist states, the highly advanced Lunars are the bankers of the Solar System, "peaceful" merchants willing to knock invading ships from the skies with mighty massdriver weapons.

The Asteroid Belt

A scattered anarchy of tumbling planetoids and rough rock miners, where every sentient has the right to vote, and the majority rules among five hundred miniature worlds.

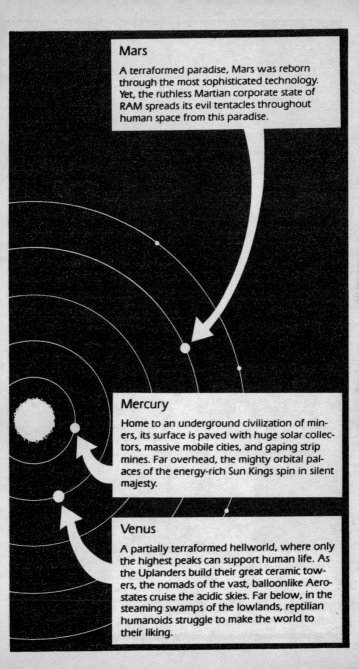

Mars

A terraformed paradise, Mars was reborn through the most sophisticated technology. Yet, the ruthless Martian corporate state of RAM spreads its evil tentacles throughout human space from this paradise.

Mercury

Home to an underground civilization of miners, its surface is paved with huge solar collectors, massive mobile cities, and gaping strip mines. Far overhead, the mighty orbital palaces of the energy-rich Sun Kings spin in silent majesty.

Venus

A partially terraformed hellworld, where only the highest peaks can support human life. As the Uplanders build their great ceramic towers, the nomads of the vast, balloonlike Aerostates cruise the acidic skies. Far below, in the steaming swamps of the lowlands, reptilian humanoids struggle to make the world to their liking.

Chapter One

A staggering movement made the flexible framework of the huge laboratory shift as a robotic arm swung slowly around, its jaws clutching a fitting. Carefully it rotated the fitting as it moved toward the aperture growing on the floor of the laboratory, whining in a hum of oiled machinery. The fitting was octagonal, with a hole in the center, for all the world like an old-fashioned nut without the screw threads. Instead, there were holes drilled in the center of each flat section.

"Careful! You be careful, Matt Kinswept! I warned you before, an' I'll say it again—watch your level switch! Your level switch, you idiot!"

The foreman bawled orders through his communications link at a man standing in a high cage, manipulating levers. Matt Kinswept was a top robotics man, but the unit he was handling was huge, and the controls took some getting used to. He kept his eyes glued to the monitor screen and the fitting's destination as he nudged the directional controls. Suddenly the jaws wobbled. The fitting careened crazily. Kinswept caressed the level switch and the wobble stabilized. "So you saw that coming," he muttered at his still bellowing supervisor.

The huge laboratory workroom was attached like a cocoon to one of the Mariposa solar satellites, which circled the planet Mercury. It was an insignificant cylindrical blemish on the apex of the satellite's central core, hardly noticeable in the complicated framework of the solar collector.

Kinswept kept the crane moving. As it neared the floor, its movements became invisible to the naked eye. As gently as a mother placing a baby in its crib, Kinswept lowered the fitting into the octagonal housing at the center of the aperture. The two slipped together, and the operation was complete.

The foreman let the air whistle through his teeth in a sigh of relief. "All right, now," he bawled. "You see what I tell you? She's a wobbler! You got to watch her all the time. We lose one—just one—of these here fittings, and you can kiss your vacation good-bye."

"Sure, sure," said the operator. He released the vise-grip jaws and lifted the crane away from the aperture.

Once the framework was clear, a welder's cage swung toward the structure. It hovered inches from the seam between housing and fitting. The welder, his safety harness securing him to the cage, sat on the makeshift cross-brace made of inch-thick alloy. Sparks would wash off it like water. A torch could cut it, but it would not burn. He pulled his face shield down, made a thumbs-up gesture to the foreman, and hit the switch on his welding torch.

Blue flame shot out in a twelve-inch-wide sheet that disappeared into the crack between the housing and fitting. The welder watched the metal change color, then manipulated the controls on his torch so the flame eased down the crack like butter. The work was painstaking, but it left behind a seam so fine it was hard to see.

Gordon Gavilan watched the placement of the first crystal holder through a pair of powerful binoculars. He was a broad, heavily built man, his initially handsome face marred by years of dissipation. His hair and clipped beard were streaked with white, but his brown eyes were as sharp and ruthless as they had been in his youth. He wore his thickly embroidered brown suit with an air and sat in a chamber of clear panels set in a gold alloy framework. The supports for the panels were braided rods of gold. Climbing the braids were white-gold vines flowering into occasional explosions of glittering squash blossoms. Gordon's chair was heavily padded with wine-colored cushions. It fit the contours of his powerful body like a glove, for it was built to the exact physical specifications of this heir to the fabulously wealthy Sun Kings of Mercury.

Gordon had ordered the chamber's construction on the day he approved the plans for the laser, intending to watch the fulfillment of his dreams of power. In his gilded cage, he hovered above the project. To the men in his employ, he was a vulture waiting for a mistake, and his gimlet eyes cut the ranks down early. In his own heart, he was a father ensuring the life of his child.

The uprising on Earth, which, against all odds, freed the home planet from Martian domination, had rocked Gordon to his soul. It destroyed an established order of Martian superiority that dated back decades. It had proved the fragility of political institutions. In that uprising, Gordon Gavilan saw seeds of discord that threatened the security of Mercury, and, more important, the security of the Gavilan house.

Gavilans had ruled the wealth of Mercury for a very long time. Their initiative in constructing the Mariposa satellites, and the wealth those power stations generated, had made a secure foundation of political control essentially unchallenged to this day. Yet Gordon was afraid. He was a student of history. He knew that the success of one rebellion fomented others, sparks of dissatisfaction that turned the dry tinder of the underprivileged soul into a flame of destruction.

He was fully aware that Mercury contained fertile ground for such unrest. It had never erupted, because of the Sun Kings' wealth. Their money could subdue a thousand rebellions on planets larger than Mercury, and the inhabitants of the warrens, those underground settlements that honeycombed the strata below Mercury's inhospitable surface—not to mention the Desert Dancers, who roamed that surface in their mobile track cities—knew it. Still, there was

magic in an ancient swashbuckling hero such as
Buck Rogers. Rogers's leadership had spearheaded
the rebellion on Earth. One of his compatriots might
yet attempt it on Mars.

Gordon set down the binoculars. His eyes were
tired, strained from watching the flame seal the two
sections of metal. He settled into the cushions, his
thoughts in a fever. Rogers reminded him of his
nephew, Kemal. Kemal was the son of Ossip, his
long-dead humanitarian brother and previous ruler
of Mercury. Gordon had raised Kemal—or seen to his
raising. He had the boy educated at the most expensive and exclusive military academy on Mars, the
preferred alma mater of many a statesman. In Kemal Gavilan the academy found a mind like a sponge
and a tough, athletic body. Kemal took the military
training well, his marks a credit to the Gavilan
name, and Gordon thought little about him until Kemal flouted his uncle's authority and joined the
rebels of NEO in their desperate fight to free Earth.

He had been enraged by Kemal's disobedience, and
even more outraged by the loss of the hereditary link
with the Desert Dancers. Kemal's father had left his
son a legacy of trust, making Kemal spokesman for
the Dancers in the Gavilan court. Kemal had not chosen to turn that honor over to his uncle. With the
recklessness of youth, he had flown in his uncle's
face, declaring that the Dancers had rights to be
respected.

It was true that the boy had come home after the
Martian Wars older, more sober. It was true that he
had finally seen the light concerning his precious
desert rats, yet he had fought on the side of NEO

against his own family, against his cousin Dalton. If there could be a black sheep in a family, there could be a black sheep in a kingdom. Gordon Gavilan did not intend to suffer either.

Instead, he had found a way to safeguard what was his, and what would belong to his heirs, for all time. He had discovered a weapon, a powerful weapon. Its existence would be a deterrent to insurrection as well as external attack. Gordon regarded the scraggly beginnings of the laser affectionately. When it was completed, it would be capable of focusing a beam of light so destructive that principalities would quail before it. Mercury's proximity to the Sun assured it the maximum power potential for the lens.

As for a rotten apple in the family barrel . . . well, either the bad spot would be cut out of it, or it would be eliminated. In any case, the laser would be programmed to Gordon's own voice print, so ultimate power would be his.

The cage vibrated as the arm swung around again, reaching for the second crystal housing. Kinswept opened the giant vise-grips delicately, lowered them over the housing, and closed them around it. The arm sailed majestically upward, then swept toward the aperture on the floor, its movements more sure as Kinswept got the feel of the equipment. Gordon Gavilan leaned forward once more, binoculars raised. The foreman estimated that they would be able to set one housing and fitting every two hours. Gavilan had ordered him to work around the clock, dangling a fat bonus under his nose as incentive.

"Congratulations, Father. Your project is under way."

Gordon glanced at his son Dalton, seated on his right. "You sound disinterested," he replied, his voice hard. "This project concerns you, of all people. It is your security."

Gordon's estimation of his son was incorrect. Dalton's pride was expressed in verbal apathy. He had been removed from command of Rising Sun Station, where the initial research on the laser had been conducted. Bitterest of all, he had been replaced by his cousin Kemal. He nursed anger. "I find better security in a fleet of fast ships, armed with the latest technology," he said.

"You are a superb warrior, Dalton, but sometimes you amaze me. Are you so short-sighted you do not know where the resources to finance your fleet come from?" Gordon turned his uncompromising eyes on Dalton.

"I may be a man of action, but I am not a fool, Father. I am well aware my fleet owes its existence to the Mariposas." Dalton shifted in his seat, his powerful physique a younger, trimmer version of his father's. Lowering black brows and a shock of black hair gave his face a brooding look. His black eyes were shadowed, his square face lean.

"And to the money they bring in, money which has been in our family for generations and which I do not intend to lose. Rebellion is blowing across the system like a solar wind. I feel it. It whispers to the people of Mercury that Gavilan money might be theirs. It sings to our enemies that Mercury is ripe for the picking. I will make those winds die."

Dalton arched a heavy black eyebrow at his father. The Gavilans were raised to political paranoia. They were trained to suspect their own motives, let alone the intentions of those around them. Intrigue ran in their blood, but even so, Dalton thought his father was reaching for specters. "Last report from Rabbit in the warrens?" he drawled.

Gordon shook his head. "No. The warrens are quiet—according to Rabbit."

"His information has always been reliable," commented Dalton.

"This is not about the warrens or the track cities! I am talking about other possibilities, Dalton!"

"You are jumping at shadows," said Dalton bluntly. Few other men on Mercury would have dared address Gordon so.

"Perhaps." Gordon's voice was steel. "And perhaps not. As I see it, I am ensuring the future of the Gavilan family, and through us the domination of Mercury Prime over the planet. The laser will be our watchdog, warning off intrusion and threats."

"And the consequences?" Dalton's mouth barely moved around the words. "Have you considered them? Have you considered the possibility, however remote, that someone might use the laser?"

Gordon's hand swung out and back like a boomerang. "Impossible. We are talking about the destruction of entire regions."

"That's right."

"Not even a madman—"

"Would use it?" asked Dalton. "If I have learned one thing, Father, it is that there are those in this world willing to commit suicide to injure another. I am a practical man. I would not choose such a course, but there are those who would." Dalton's bitterness

ARRIVAL

THE MARTIAN WARS TRILOGY

Book One: Rebellion 2456
Book Two: Hammer of Mars
Book Three: Armageddon Off Vesta

THE INNER PLANETS TRILOGY

Volume One: First Power Play
Volume Two: Prime Squared
Volume Three: Matrix Cubed

Kemal Gavilan would not pay under any court system on Mercury for the wrong he had done the Dancers or the humiliation he had heaped upon Duernie. If he were to be brought to justice, it would be by her hand. Duernie extracted a knife from the sheath on her leg. Its wide blade glittered, even in the diffused light of the duct. She ran a finger along its cutting edge, testing it.

The blade's glitter was hypnotizing, full of rainbows and refracted light. She found it beautiful. It was a symbol of the justice she craved. With it a man might be cut down to size. He would no longer be a member of a privileged group. He would be a man begging for life, and he would be begging it of her.

D1569984

erupted in the force of his words.

"And that is why," replied Gordon, "I have restricted control of the laser. It will activate to my voiceprint alone. When the time comes, power will be transferred to my successor."

Dalton did not lose the implication in his father's words. No matter how serious the conversation, Gordon could not resist playing political games. Not for one moment did Dalton consider the possibility that his father might award power to another. "It is a wise precaution, Father."

"Yes." Gordon's reply was absent. The robot arm had manipulated the housing into position on the aperture and was returning for the octagonal fitting. He watched the machine in fascination, thinking of the legends from old Earth, of prehistoric behemoths, beasts with long necks and powerful jaws, that towered above puny humans. His fancy clothed the arm's steel framework in flesh and blood, gave it color and form. The fancy pleased him, and he made a mental note to commit the image to poetry.

Dalton leaned back, his black brows drawn together in concentration. He had not wanted to accompany his father on this inspection. It was a stinging reminder of the humiliation of Rising Sun. But, on reflection, he was glad he had come. Gordon had ruled Mercury Prime ably for many years, but he was no longer a young man. Age . . . altered perspective. Perhaps the time was nearing when his father would enjoy a well-earned rest.

Chapter Two

The Eye of Phidias belonged to the Desert Dancers. Located deep at the bottom of a circular vent, it glowed like a miniature reflection of the Sun. The vent ran a quarter mile straight down, and the rising steam from the pool of molten magma was dissipated by the time it reached Mercury's surface, so that it was a disturbance in the air, a shimmer in the Sun's baking rays. The Eye was visible only by overflying it.

A decade ago, a lone wildcatter had sent his skimmer over the vent slowly enough for the mining detectors to pick up readings of the flowing rock. The miner had reported it, but markets in the warrens deemed it an unlikely risk. The depth of the fissure made cost-effective mining procedures impossible. The Eye of Phidias was marked on the charts as a curiosity and ceded to the Dancers as worthless.

So it had been until another independent miner named Madog had stumbled through the narrow canyon that linked the Eye to the rest of Phidias Basin. Madog found a cluster of crystal formations. Each crystal stood taller than a man. The blossom of angular petals caught the harsh sunlight and turned it into glowing rainbows so beautiful that they stopped the heart. Red and orange and lavender and saffron and blue and green—green that Mercurians knew from pictures of terraformed worlds—blazed from every petal. Madog, awed by their beauty, called them "Sun Flowers." It was he who discovered that the crystals glowed in the freezing Mercurian dark, glowed with the stored warmth and color of the Sun. Stranded in the fissure, the warmth of the crystals saved his life.

Ubrahil Carrera brought the plans for a commercial crystal farm to Mercury. Crystals were being successfully produced on Venus. Their quality was mediocre, but the price made them a profitable investment. Though currently a relatively rare commodity, research showed that crystals could be used in everything from medical lasers to propulsion units. They could focus power, boosting output and profits. Carrera was not a man to skirt opportunity.

The son of a moderately successful surface miner, Carrera was Dancer born and bred. He had fought and scratched with the best of them to wrest a living from Mercury. When his father died, leaving him a modest inheritance, Carrera vowed that he would build it into a secure fortune that would enable him to forsake the Dancers' nomadic existence. He had used his money to purchase the rights to the Eye of Phidias.

His family and friends had questioned his sanity, but he paid them no mind. Instead, he had opened up the one narrow fissure leading to the Eye. He sent a crew in to construct a fan plateau, a kind of pie-shaped strip mine created by extensive slicing of the planet's surface. The apex of the pie was the Eye, and by the time the equipment departed, replete with ore, Carrera's pockets were full of cash and the Eye lay exposed to easy approach.

He built a radiation dome beside it and used his profits from the mining operation to buy equipment. He hired a skeleton crew, all Dancers used to the rigors of the surface, imported a technical staff of three, and set about growing crystals. His success promised to be phenomenal. In six short months of operation, the Eye of Phidias Crystal Field was producing crystals of unusual size and uniformity. The first specimens to be placed on the open market had brought prime rates.

The remaining natural crystals Carrera had left standing. They had become a part of Dancer culture, a symbol of beauty and survival. It pleased Carrera that his artificially grown crystals would make the harvesting of the natural crystal bed unnecessary.

Carrera's thin lips curved in satisfaction. He was a tall man with dark brown radiation-burned, pock-marked skin. His high cheekbones rose above dramatic hollows, and his tapering jaw was bony. He had a thin beak of a nose and brown eyes that should have been soulful but were half-closed in a permanent squint from too much sunlight. He wore loose scarlet robes, with a twisted piece of red-and-white cloth knotted at the back of his head to keep his long hair away from his face. One gold earring glittered in his left ear.

"The delegation has arrived," announced Carrera's manservant.

Carrera's smile expanded, showing crooked white teeth. He did not look at his servant as he replied, "Show them to the solar dome."

"At once," replied the servant, bowing out of the room.

Carrera waited patiently, giving the delegation time to settle into the relative comfort of the solar dome. He wanted to make an entrance, and to do that he needed a slightly bored and irritated audience. He gave the delegation ten minutes of frustration before he crossed the courtyard from his living quarters to the reception area. He had built himself a modest but comfortable home in the wall of Phidias Basin. Below the planet's surface, he was protected from the harsh Mercurian climate. His reception area was his link to the outside. He had installed thick, transparent panels that allowed him a view of the planet's surface, for his Dancer heritage craved the stark beauty of the harsh landscape.

He swept into the solar dome, his robes swirling about him. The delegation stood before him like ninepins, straight and uniform in their life suits, face shields thrown back. Through the transparent panels behind them, Carrera could see their skimmers.

Jet powered, they were highly fuel efficient, capable of extended travel, a modern mechanical version of the old Earth camel.

"Welcome to the Eye of Phidias," said Carrera, one hand moving in a sweeping gesture toward the far side of the room.

The movement was a signal. The top half of the wall split in the center and fell back toward the adjoining walls in thin triangular sections. The visitors were treated to a panoramic view of the crystal farm through a gigantic computer viewscreen. One of the delegates gasped. It was no wonder. The screen held a stupendous sight. Row after row of crystals sparkled in every color of the rainbow, from jewel hues to crackling clarity to velvet black.

"Really, Ubrahil, your theatrics are wasted on us," said a delegate dryly. He was a man of indeterminate years. His head was bald, but he made up for it with a sweeping mustache that curled up at the ends in perfect circles.

"Really?" answered Carrera. "The sight always thrills me. Look how they catch the light! Mercury is an unforgiving world, but I have wrested these flowers from her." He turned abruptly away from the crystal beds. "I understand you gentlemen wish to inspect the farm."

"All right, Ubrahil. I'll say it. Uncle. We all thought you were crazy. It appears you were as crazy as a Venusian crocfox. There's money to be made here, and not just by you. The few crystals you have sold to art dealers have brought prosperity. A larger market based on artificially grown crystals means wealth. I think we are looking at the Dancers' ticket to independence from Gavilan domination."

"That's a heavy political statement, Alain Robbin.
I didn't think you could put words of that length
together."

"I deserve that. I've been one of your biggest crit-
ics. That's why I'm here—to swallow my pride, to see
if crystal farming is practical without a magma
pool."

Carrera's eyes became slits. "Why now?" he asked.
"And why me? The technical expertise for my operation is no secret. You could buy it anywhere."

"That's true, but we could not buy it in time. There
are rumors, Ubrahil, of Gavilan interest in crystals.
We are here to offer you the protection of the track
cities."

"You think the Sun King will raid my farm?" Carrera's voice was amused.

"You may laugh, but the Eye of Phidias does not
move. Its location is no secret. The Gavilans had
Duernie followed to the Eye. What will prevent Gavilan from taking what he wants instead of buying it?"
asked Robbin.

"The desire for a continued supply, for one thing,"
replied Carrera. "Duernie? The liaison with Kemal
Gavilan?"

Robbin inclined his head.

Carrera studied him shrewdly. "You mean none of
this. What is your real purpose here?"

A short woman stepped out from behind Robbin. In
spite of his intentions, Carrera bowed.

"Rise, Ubrahil Carrera. We are not in council now."
Corianne, the second ranked official on the council of
the Desert Dancers, advanced another step. "We are

here to beg your help. You are becoming a rich man,
Carrera. In riches lies power. The Gavilans taught us
that centuries ago. It is time we broke free of their
domination. Always our livelihood has hinged on
chance, the discovery of a rich vein or lode. In your
crystal farm, I see for the first time a way of controlling our destiny instead of being driven by the desert
winds."

"You really expect me to support competition?"

"Yes."

"Why?" Carrera was baffled by Corianne's words.

"Because you are a Desert Dancer. Because the
song of the desert is stronger than blood, stronger
even than greed. Because we have been pawns too
long." She raised her tawny brown eyes, clear in spite
of her years, in a challenge.

Carrera met her look squarely, but his squint
creased until his eyes were black slits in his angular
face.

Suddenly Corianne nodded, a short affirmation.
"Now, brother," she said, "what percentage of the
crystals we see here are dependent on the Eye?"

Carrera smiled in spite of himself. She was his master, and amusement at his own pretension made his
mobile mouth arch. He answered lightly, in accord
with the heritage she represented. "We have used
the Eye as the center of our operation. The vapors are
piped to sealed chambers, where they are precisely
regulated. We are becoming more and more adept at
controlling pressure and the chemical mix. You will
see the pipes running along the outside edge of the
farm."

"And the magma?" asked Robbin.

"That is more difficult to handle, but it looks as if it will be worth the trouble. Some of our largest, purest crystals have been distilled from it. It can be extruded under pressure, providing more uniform and larger crystals for the industrial uses we are discovering. We are selling the vapor-generated crystals to art collectors, who value their individuality."

Carrera went to a control panel on the wall and touched it. "Hopkins, will you come in here? I have some visitors who wish to question you." He turned to the delegation. "Hopkins is a chemical engineer. The Eye of Phidias was developed under his orders."

Hopkins entered the solar dome with brisk steps, a touch of annoyance in the set of his mouth. He was a chemist, not a diplomat, and he did not enjoy playing at public relations. His quick blue eyes took in the delegation at a glance, stopping for the merest fraction of a second on Corianne. One of his expressive eyebrows quirked, and he inclined his head. Corianne returned the courtesy with a smile.

"You have accomplished great things with the Eye of Phidias," she said. "Perhaps you will explain the principles. The council is interested in the feasibility of crystal growing on a large scale. Is a phenomenon such as the Eye requisite?"

Hopkins's annoyance eased. He liked talking about his work, even to lay persons. "No. It is merely a happy accident. It provides us with a ready-made chemical compound that happens to produce particularly fine crystals if handled correctly. However, crystals may be grown entirely artificially, using a mixture of chemicals in a laboratory."

"But that is hardly profitable," voiced a delegate.

"Certainly not compared to the resources available here on Mercury. The entire planet is a warehouse of chemical riches." A twinkle glinted in Hopkins's eyes.

"Then it is not unreasonable to see a future in crystal farming?" asked Corianne.

Hopkins shook his head. "Hardly. Especially with the proposed use of crystals in farming. The cold planets are beginning to experiment with solar greenhouses. Crystal boosters could significantly increase their efficiency. Then there is the transportation industry. Anywhere it is an advantage to concentrate power, crystals can be used, and, since they do not last forever, the demand will always exceed the supply."

"They do not last?" asked one of the delegates, a tall man with disapproving features.

"No," replied Hopkins. "Channeling power through the crystals takes its toll. Eventually they darken, and that reduces their efficiency. In the end, they may break down completely. In laboratory experiments, I have seen crystals crack into dust under excessive stress."

"And that is their great gift," said Carrera. "There is no wealth in a commodity that lasts forever. There is wealth in a necessary component that must be replaced at regular intervals. Do you think I invested my money without study? I assure you, I analyzed the market carefully."

"Let me show you the operation," Hopkins offered. "Then you will better understand the feasibility of growing crystals on Mercury. Notice the chambers."

"They are full of fog," said Alain Robbin.

"Yes. That is the natural chemical vapor rising from the Eye. We trap it, pipe it into the chambers until it reaches a precise level of concentration, and then begin the serious business of growing crystals." Hopkins launched into an explanation of the process, enthusiasm bubbling in his voice as he progressed.

Corianne, standing next to Ubrahil Carrera, observed the explanation with detachment. She was preoccupied by information the others overlooked. "You mentioned sales," she said.

"Yes," answered Carrera. He nodded. "So far, most of our crystals have gone to art collectors."

"You are sure of this?" asked Corianne.

"Yes. Why?"

"There are, as Robbin suggested, indications of Gavilan interest. Gordon is reputed to possess a fine art collection. It is said he keeps several auction houses solvent. I merely wonder what he is up to," said Corianne.

"Who can fathom the Gavilan mind?" answered Carrera.

The look Corianne gave him was reproving. "You will do well to study his intentions. We Dancers have learned again the painful reality of dealing with the Gavilans. Trust is not a word they understand."

"They do understand profit," replied Ubrahil.

"Perhaps. But only for themselves. How do you know Gordon Gavilan will not let you develop this crystal farm, pour your life and your money into it, and, if he finds it expedient, snatch it from you as if he were taking toys from a baby?"

A shadow crossed Carrera's angular face. "I had not considered that."

"We trusted Kemal Gavilan. We believed his pro-
testations of friendship, and he betrayed us without a
thought. He betrayed Duernie, who saved his life. He
lived with us! Even that did not stop him." Corianne's
elderly hands, with protruding veins and thick
joints, fluttered in a surprisingly graceful gesture of
futility.

"I do not trust Gordon Gavilan. And there is this.
The Gavilans may be ruthless, but they have never
really interfered in Dancer business. They have let
us prospect the planet, and they have profited from
our discoveries."

"While we live in poverty," put forth a shorter delegate.

Carrera nodded. "But, they have been content to
let us do the work."

Corianne spoke quietly. "I do not trust a stationary
installation. It is too easy to find, too easy to destroy."

"Spoken like a true Dancer," said Carrera with a
smile.

"We have wandered the deserts of Mercury for un-
counted years," answered Corianne. "I do not dispute
the possibility of change. However, I do not find it
easy."

"Yet you are here," said Carrera.

"Yes. I am here," Corianne sighed. "To learn about
a new way of life that seems to be better than the old.
Yet I find my heart yearning for the blasted plains
and my feet itching to seek the horizon. Change may
often be good, but it is never easy."

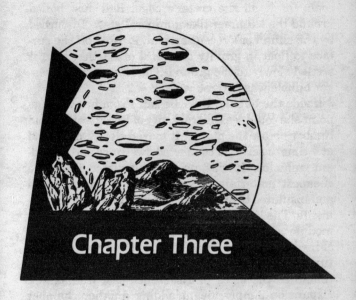

Chapter Three

The harsh sunlight of Mercury swept across the barren red desert in a wash of blazing light along the leading edge of Darkside. The pock-marked plain was a wasteland of sand and rubble, vast oceans of it between the craters. The craters themselves rose in wrinkled rims high into the Mer-curian sky. They were circular mountains of varying sizes. Many of them bore signs of mining operations, but humans' pathetic hen-scratches barely marred the surface of the mineral-rich world.

Far from the Eye of Phidias, on the uneven rim of a small crater, a Dancer skimmer was parked under the shadow of sheltering darkness. There was just room for it on the crater's edge. Red dust boiled around the skimmer like a mineral stew. Disturbed by the skimmer's recent arrival, it lifted off the surface to float in gravity one-third of Earth's, then it settled slowly to the ground. The skimmer's passenger bubble was covered with it.

Inside the bubble, Duernie sat. From her vantage point she could see the track city of Renaissance Gold lumber across the planet. It moved slowly, one tread at a time, a series of connected dwellings and attendant vehicles. It was ugly. Constructed from the cheapest materials, it was largely metal, shielded and insulated to protect the inhabitants from the elements. The life-support systems were built into each module and were attached like tumors to the machined and riveted skin. Because there was no moisture to corrupt the metal, it did not rust, but remained the black of a seasoned cast iron skillet. Expansion simply meant adding another chamber and another set of tracks. Because of the dust their movements threw up, the tracks were obscured. The city appeared to float slowly over the planet's surface like a glowering metal monster.

The dour feeling of track cities was mirrored in the severe outlook of the Dancers themselves. Despite their penchant for art, music, and storytelling, they were not a people given to frivolity of spirit. Their lives were too hard. Even their art was serious business, and Duernie was true to her heritage. Her long, dark hair was pulled severely back from her bronze face. She had braided it, then twisted the braid into a figure eight, which she pinned at the back of her head with a gold ornament. Her brown suit fit her well, but was loose enough for comfort. At her belt she carried a mono knife, the hilt a gold panther, its mouth open as it leapt for its prey. Enameled black spots followed the beast's contours, and its eyes were topaz. Thrown over the skimmer's passenger seat was a dark brown cloak, its bright yellow lining a splash of brilliant color against the drab interior.

Duernie watched the track city move, her dark eyes unreadable, her face stone. She stared at it, but she did not see it. It was a picture moving before her, no more real than the image on a computer screen. It was an approximation of life, not life itself, just as Kemal Gavilan's friendship had been an approximation. She had believed him! That ground into her soul. She, Duernie, known for her distance and cynicism, had believed a Gavilan.

Kemal's face lingered in her mind. He was all exciting Gavilan looks, though without the dramatic contrasts of his uncle Gordon or cousin Dalton. Their black hair and colorful clothes made them noticeable in a crowd. Kemal was not. His brown hair, golden bronze skin, and plainly cut clothes made him less a king and more a man. In his hazel eyes there lurked an edge of danger. Duernie knew now that it could become a devil. His winning smile and indifference to the relative hardships of the track, his military background and physical prowess, had eventually gained him Dancer trust.

Because he had refused to cede the Dancers' voice to his uncle, because he had chosen exile with the Dancers over the riches of the Gavilan court, she had thought him different. She had thought him sincere. She closed her eyes, and the memories flooded her an-

gry mind. She could feel Kemal's arms around her,
their satin-steel strength enclosing her. She had relaxed into them in a moment of vulnerability, knowing he was the only man she had ever really wanted.

He had treated her as a friend, and for that she had
been his spokesman with the Dancers. He had joined
NEO to fight for the freedom of Earth, for the individual freedom of its inhabitants. Freedom was not
something the Gavilan mind readily understood, but
Kemal had seemed to understand it. For that she had
loved him, though she had never spoken a word.

When Huer, Buck Rogers's personal digital personality, had begged her help in locating and freeing Kemal from his uncle's dungeons, Duernie had
complied. She and Kemal had been through moments of crackling danger together. He had let her
see some of his fear, some of his pain. For Duernie,
that was a courage she had not experienced. Of all
things, she protected her weakness from the eyes of
others. Kemal had handed his to her, trusting her.

The memories cut like a knife in her vitals. She
loved him. She could not kill that love, in spite of his
actions, and that hurt worst of all. He had betrayed
the Dancers' trust, thrown their hospitality and
friendship back in their faces, and joined his clan, yet
she could not kill the love. He had used Duernie,
duped her into betraying the location of Ubrahil Carrera's crystal farm. Anger at her weakness was a
black storm that raged through Duernie's soul.

A roar like a disturbed volcano rumbled over her
head. Duernie looked up through the dusty bubble of
her skimmer to see a huge freighter. Its docking
lights blinked blue against Mercurian red. She

placed it on course for the warrens. The warrens made a fat living off ship repair. Mercury was the most approachable of the planets sunward. Even large vessels could dock and take off with little loss of efficiency. The warrens traded on this, doing a thriving business. Their mechanics were considered as good as any in the system, and the warrens themselves thrived on the traffic, entertaining visiting crews. Duernie picked up the end of the approach conversation on her communications system.

"Warren Watch, this is Pack Mule I, out from Venus. We have developed power loss on our rear thruster unit. We've got stabilization problems, Warren Watch. Nearly took out a Mariposa . . ." The transmission crackled as the ship disappeared over the horizon.

Duernie smiled. The thought of one of the Gavilans' precious money machines being destroyed by a passing vessel was a balm to her soul. Kemal had proved his loyalties, and with them the priorities he held most dear: Gavilan priorities of money and power. The only way to hurt a Gavilan was in the pocketbook.

And Duernie wanted to hurt Gavilans, in retaliation for the humiliation they had heaped on her people, but most of all for the betrayal she had suffered at Kemal's hands. For that, he should pay in the coin that would hurt him most: profit.

Her memories of the sabotage she and Kemal had performed on the Mariposas were vivid. The orbiting solar collectors were the source of Gavilan wealth, the basis on which the empire was constructed. Losing even one of them would wound the Gavilan spirit.

She considered the consequences of guerrilla action. The Gavilans were entirely capable of blasting the track cities from the face of Mercury. They boasted a sizable space fleet, and their home space station, Mercury Prime—called Hielo by some—not to mention numerous satellites, gave them the surveillance capability of launching a devastating attack from space. The Dancers were vulnerable.

The desire for vengeance burned in Duernie's soul. The Mariposas were a tempting target. If a strike could be arranged to look like an accident, she might accomplish her goal without incurring Gavilan wrath for her people. She hugged the idea to her, cherishing it. All she needed was a derelict ship or a malfunctioning satellite. She mulled over impossible ways and means, vengeance building in her soul, an intoxication more deadly than any she had ever known.

Chapter Four

The spacer staggered backward, his arms flailing helplessly, hands grabbing wildly at the empty air. Overbalanced by a tremendous shove, he could not stop himself. He hit the sensitive electronic door controls, and the slabs of metal opened behind him like a camera lens. The open eye revealed Black Barney, his seven-foot frame entirely blocking the exit. The spacer crashed into him.

With a snarl of annoyance, Barney picked the gennie up and threw him back into the bar. The spacer fell into the fight from which he had previously been ejected, knocking one of the combatants to the floor and stunning the other. There was a momentary lull in the conversation as patrons waited for action. When it did not come, they resumed talking. The three troublemakers lay groaning in the center of the floor.

"Drag 'em out," ordered the proprietor, a fat man with a towel stuck into his belt.

His head bobbing like an antique toy, a servant scuttled toward the pile, grabbed the spacer by one foot, and began to drag him toward the door. The spacer's protests were weak, and the servant, a short, solid gennie engineered for manual labor, paid him no mind.

Barney stepped over the remaining two bodies with fine indifference. Black Barney was a gennie himself, one of the infamous Barney series. Seven feet of rock-hard bone and muscle, Barney's physical prowess was staggering. His natural gifts were enhanced by retractable cybernetic wrist knives. He was a killing machine with no conscience or morals. He knew one law: loyalty to a captain, a man he acknowledged as his superior.

For Black Barney, master pirate, that man was Buck Rogers. He owed Rogers allegiance because the twentieth century hero had bested him. He answered to no one else. He had fought with Rogers in the Martian Wars, not because he believed in NEO's cause or because he wanted to free the home planet, but because Buck asked him to help. He would fight again for Rogers, because he knew Buck could kill him. Still, if the truth were known, Barney had a sneaking affection for his captain. It was not an emotion that would hamper his actions, should Buck ever lose the pirate's loyalty, but it made service less onerous.

Barney's tortured face, with its colorless eyes, was a vision that haunted the dreams of many of his victims. He wore a complete suit of black body armor. Like the Roman armor of old Earth, it was contoured in a sculptural representation of the muscles it protected. Under the flickering blue lights and smoky haze of the Pendragon Cantina, it gleamed.

Without a word, Barney swaggered over to the bar, placed a huge elbow on it, and stared the proprietor down.

The man was wiping a glass, but one look from Barney made him swallow his tongue. He gulped, then finally managed, "What can I get you?"

Barney looked at him. He enjoyed the exercise of fear.

"Whatever your honor wants," supplemented the bartender.

"Ginger beer," said Barney casually.

The bartender choked the hysterical laugh that rose in his throat. He reached for his largest tumbler, fumbled, then set it on the bar. He poured a foaming glass of ginger beer and pushed the drink toward Barney.

The pirate picked up the glass in his huge fist, raised it, then tossed it off in three swallows. He slammed the tumbler down. "Another!" he demanded.

The bartender poured, not daring to ask for payment. Barney consumed three glasses before he tossed down a credit. The bartender snatched it, lest his irascible patron decide to take it back. With a fourth drink clutched in his fist, Barney turned away from the bar and glowered at the other customers.

They were a noisy lot. The space station Tortuga, off Venus, was a free marketplace. Like the asteroid belt, it was a haven for the scum of the spaceways. The colony survived on vice, pleasure gennies, and a thriving black market. On Tortuga, the rules were few. A person could do what he or she wanted.

The Pendragon Cantina was a favorite of spacers and other gennies. As Barney looked around the room, he saw a high percentage of workers, those gennies designed to do the most menial chores throughout the solar system. They had little in the way of brains, but they were physically strong. They also were small, the better to fit into the confines of long-term space flight, and as tough as nails. They had no hair. Their rough, leathery skin was a distinct shade of yellow. Their eyes were small and dark, their mouths wide and thick.

In the far corner of the cantina was a different class of patron. Barney could smell other pirates, no matter what their disguises, and these men were not in disguise. Glasses clanked and bursts of uproarious laughter testified to their enjoyment. Interspersed with masculine roars were the high-pitched giggles of female pleasure gennies. Barney sauntered over to the group.

The first man caught sight of him, and the laughter died on his face. He grabbed the scantily clad pleasure gennie next to him, pulling her away from the group, and disappeared. The opening his departure made gave Barney a clear look at the center of the group. Seated with the back of his chair propped against the wall was another Barney. Black Barney's taciturn features split in a grin that had nothing to

do with welcome. Here was an adversary worth taking on.

Sattar Tabibi came from the same bioengineered
series as Black Barney, but he approached piracy in a
more jovial manner. Tabibi had enjoyed the fruits of
his thievery. Seated on one of his huge legs was a red-
headed pleasure gennie. Her heart-shaped face
pouted desire, and her blue eyes were half-lidded,
dark with promise. She wore a transparent body
stocking dusted with silver sparkles on all the right
places. She looked at Black Barney from under her
red thatch, teasing him, but Barney was immune.

Tabibi chuckled as he slapped the girl's thigh. "You
never did know how to have fun!" he said to Barney
casually.

Barney growled. "Have my own fun," he replied.
"Like tearin' off your head."

Tabibi chuckled again. He was as broad as Barney,
but not as tall, missing the master pirate's stature by
only two inches. His joviality was a show. "In your
dreams," he said. "Still, it doesn't hurt to have fantasies." He ran his hand down the girl's leg, and she
squirmed closer to him.

"Mrrr," snarled Barney.

The redhead played with Tabibi's long brown hair,
her teeth sunk into her full lower lip in concentration. Pleasure gennies were not often bred for brains.
Tabibi regarded her affectionately. She suited his
needs, and needed no worry. When he was gone, she
would transfer to another. He gave her a squeeze and
was rewarded with a seductive wriggle.

"Now me," said Tabibi, "I've been doing just fine."

"Um," answered Barney. He knew Tabibi needed

no encouragement to brag, and he wanted to hear
what his clone brother had to say. Barney had left Kemal Gavilan on Mercury Prime, satisfied to have
seen Kemal home. His crew was restless, hungry for
the spoils of serious pirating, but Barney had left
Mercury with a single question pounding in his
skull. Who had killed Hugo Dracolysk and stolen the
Gavilans' experimental laser? He had a feeling Tabibi was about to tell him.

"Just fine," Tabibi repeated.

"Theft," said Barney.

Tabibi nodded. "Class ten theft."

Barney regarded him sardonically. Bragging was
bragging, but the laser theft rated less than a nine.
"Eight," he said.

"As I said," answered Tabibi. "Class ten. Stole it
right out from under the Gavilans' noses." He chuckled again, coldly. "And I hear there was a dividend."
Tabibi's eyes were bright with the memory. He
smiled, a smile so chilling that the redhead tried to
pull away from him.

"Dividend." Barney made the word a statement.

"An execution," said Tabibi.

"Mmmm," said Barney expressively. "Hugo
Dracolysk."

Hugo Dracolysk had been the black-hearted
founder of Dracolysk Corporation, the organization
that had created and trained the Barneys. The training methods had been beyond vicious, torture designed to drain the warrior gennies' souls of all
humanity. Eventually, Dracolysk's creations had
risen against him and destroyed his operations.

Now, years later, one of the Barneys had finally

killed Dracolysk himself.

"Sweet operation," said Tabibi. "In—out—smooth. Snatched it so fast even you didn't know who I was," bragged Tabibi, returning to the theft to goad Barney's curiosity.

"Gavilans'll be mad," commented Barney, refusing to play Tabibi's game.

Tabibi nodded. "So they will. But what I got was worth it."

"Specialty item. You went to Valmar," said Barney, trying to draw Tabibi out.

"And she gave me a good price for it." Tabibi's empty eyes glittered momentarily at the memory of Ardala Valmar, whose voluptuous beauty and black-widow talent for seduction made her most memorable, if dangerous. "That laser's made me a rich man. I can spend the rest of my days on Tortuga!" Tabibi's clear eyes laughed in his clone brother's face. "Face it," he said. "You'd give your blood to have been the one to kill Dracolysk. There isn't a clone brother who won't follow me now."

"Rrrrr." There was disapproval in Barney's growl.

Tabibi grinned at Barney's dour comment and twisted the knife. "I think I'm going to like being master of the Rogues' Guild."

Barney contained his temper with an effort. He himself was a leader of that band of brigands known by some as the Black Brotherhood. "Could've been master of more than that," Barney drawled.

Tabibi's eyes narrowed.

"You missed out," said Barney. "Should've kept the laser. Could've held cities for ransom with it to back you up."

Tabibi pulled the girl close, one huge hand on her
rear. He nuzzled her red hair. As much as Tabibi
hated to admit it, even to himself, Barney was right.
He had made a quick profit when he might have
made billions.

Barney, on the track of information, had no patience with Tabibi's philandering. "How'd you know
it belonged to Gavilan?" he asked. The sentence was
a strain on his usual taciturnity.

Tabibi shrugged, displacing the female gennie. She
clung to his large torso. "How else? A Gavilan ship
was in among the Dracolysk wing on Rising Sun
Station."

Barney nodded. The Gavilans, in fact all Mercurians, decorated every inch of their ships. The more
money they had, the more embellishment the ships
sported, rather like men with elaborate tattoos. Mercurian vessels were distinctive, for each family had
emblazoned its ships with the family signet.

"Dalton?" asked Barney, inquiring after the leader
of the Gavilan forces.

"His personal device was on the ship I saw." Tabibi's eyes glowed. "It seems to me you're awfully curious all of a sudden."

"Mmmpf," said Barney. "Got an interest in a
Gavilan."

"Kemal." Tabibi's voice was amused. The young no-
ble's association with the pirates was an incongruous
pact.

"You take 'em out?" Barney asked.

"Got both ships before they even knew what hit
them," said Tabibi.

"No survivors?"

Tabibi looked at his clone brother evenly. "You were there," he said.

Barney swallowed the end of his drink leisurely. He looked down at Tabibi from his full height, a black mountain of ill will. "Yes," he answered.

Tabibi shrugged. "It was a class ten. The guild will confirm it."

"Mmm."

Tabibi cocked a mocking eye at Barney. "Let's see you match it," he said.

Barney took an involuntary step toward Tabibi, then the other pirate laughed.

"You never could take a joke," he said, his huge body heaving with laughter.

Barney glared at him, disarmed by the unexpected. Tabibi continued to laugh, but the laughter was silent and it did not invade his eyes. His amusement was aroused by a bigger joke than Barney knew, for the sale of the laser to Ardala was only half of his score.

Barney slammed his glass down on the table in front of Tabibi. "Business," he said succinctly, indicating that he had more important things to do than talk about past triumphs.

Tabibi watched Black Barney depart, the crowd scattering in front of his menacing frame. "Wouldn't he be frosted," Tabibi said casually into the pleasure gennie's perfect ear, "if he knew I'd sold the plans for that laser to RAM?"

Chapter Five

Black Barney strode onto the bridge of the *Free Enterprise* like a malevolent typhoon. Here on Tortuga, the ship was operating with a skeleton crew. Barney had given the bulk of his men shore leave, and they were taking advantage of his generosity by carousing through the free port. Only Arak Konii, his sly and clever face bored, remained on the bridge, languidly monitoring the ship's systems. He lost his languor as Barney approached, and stiffened to attention.

Barney swept by him without an acknowledgment, the captain's huge frame creating a flutter of breeze in the ship's breathless atmosphere. Konii swiveled in his seat as his captain passed. "Sir?" he asked.

Barney did not reply. He reached out a powerful hand and snapped his chair around, then slumped into it. His steaming black humor was the result of excessive thought. He had pondered the information he'd obtained from Tabibi a full five minutes before coming to the conclusion that someone needed to be informed of it. The question causing his present unrest was, Who should be the recipient? Kemal Gavilan was on Mercury, and the communications barriers of that planet made the discussion of sensitive information difficult. Barney glowered out the main viewscreen, his mood as black as space. "Huer," he demanded.

Konii, used to his captain's moods, complied. He accessed the communication bank's codes for NEO, extracted Huer's personal coordinates, and programmed them into the system. "I have set up the link," he said. "Estimated response time, twenty-five seconds."

"Mmmrr," acknowledged Barney. He drummed his hand on the arm of his chair. Blows ticked off the seconds. Twenty-five came and went, and Huer did not appear. Barney exercised patience. His fingers made stippled dents in the metal chair arm.

Konii's saturnine mouth was grim, his thin face tense. He had no illusions regarding Barney's reaction. "I am programming the link again, to offset the possibility of malfunction," he said, stalling. There was no reason for Huer's tardiness, and Konii racked his brains for explanations that would save his neck. Barney's small eyes turned into clear lasers of accusation. He swung slowly around toward Konii, his black body menacing, homing in for discipline.

"Huer here," said the communications link fretfully.

Barney stopped his predatory swoop, and Konii breathed again.

"Black Barney," said the captain of the *Free Enterprise*.

"Oh." Huer's monosyllable was expressive. There was a deliberate pause, and then a flutter of sound as the holographic eye on the *Free Enterprise*'s communications station activated. The camera, microphone, and speaker combined to create a convincing illusion of life. Huer appeared, perched on the weapons console. He was slight, balding, and, at the moment, nervous. His expressive brown eyes regarded the pirate as if he were trying to assess Barney's mood. As a hologram, he was safe from Barney's physical threats, but the pirate was not a predictable being, and that ruffled Huer's chips. "You wished to speak with me?" he asked primly.

"Cap'n said I was to report to you."

"Yes." Before his departure, Buck Rogers had made Huer Barney's link to the forces of NEO.

Barney nodded. Barney was more comfortable with Huer the hologram than with his disembodied voice over the communications link.

"So?" asked Huer, prodding the pirate.

"Mmm. Information," announced Barney. "Concerns Gavilan."

"Kemal?" Huer sounded surprised. "What information?"

"Found out who stole the Gavilan laser, and where it went."

"Where did you find out?" asked Huer.

Barney held up a hand. Huer's breech of pirate etiquette was glaring, but he knew from previous experience that it was not within the hologram's programming to understand. "That's my business," he said.

"Who was it?" Barney's twisted rules irritated Huer.

"Sattar Tabibi," said Barney.

"As we surmised," reflected Huer.

Barney nodded.

"And its present owner?" asked the hologram.

"Valmar," replied Barney, his rasping voice rough.

Huer nodded. He smoothed a thin hand over his blue bodysuit. "She was a logical choice," he said. He leveled his serious eyes at Barney. "What do you propose?"

Barney shrugged. As far as he was concerned, he had performed his duty to his captain. The information, and the ball, were now in Huer's hands.

"This laser . . . what was its purpose?"

"Nobody said. Could've been used as a rock drill, but what I saw was a weapon." Barney recalled a ransacked Rising Sun Station, the Gavilans' asteroid-based research facility. The memory of the armored vehicle with the laser mounted on it was vivid.

"Weapon." Huer's voice was thoughtful. He was running theories on solar lasers through his memory, trying to extract the possibilities for military use. The data that began to accumulate was not encouraging.

The Gavilan family was not friendly with NEO, or with Earth. Only Kemal was in sympathy with the democratic ideals of the home planet. Kemal had fought on NEO's side in the Martian War, and was a friend of Buck Rogers. Huer could not accept Kemal fashioning a weapon that might be trained against the planet he had fought to free. His family, however, was another story. It was in sympathy with Mars, had fought on the Martian side of the conflict. The Gavilans would contemplate with pleasure destroying the rebel band that had bested them.

Despite their pomp and circumstance, the Gavilans were a formidable military force not to be ignored. Dalton Gavilan, Kemal's cousin and leader of the Mercurian fleet, had almost defeated NEO. The Gavilans were wily and treacherous, not to be trusted. Except Kemal. Perhaps.

Huer reflected on the known data surrounding Kemal Gavilan. Raised in exile from his home planet, given the finest Martian military education, Kemal was well suited to wage war on the forces that had trained him. He had professed little affection for Mercury, a planet he barely knew, and open rebellion against his wealthy family. His championing of the Desert Dancers' cause had resulted in a break with the family, and Kemal had fled Mercury and joined NEO's cause. Now, however, with the apparent cessation of interplanetary hostilities, he had returned to Mercury, presumably to reconcile with his family.

That was public knowledge. Privately, Huer knew of Kemal's liaison with the Rogue's Guild to try to track down the new weapon his uncle was developing. With Huer's and the pirates' help, he had traced the weapon to Rising Sun Station, where he had seen the laser's destructive potential firsthand. His cousin

Dalton had been overseeing the station when Hugo Dracolysk's forces attacked. In the conflict, Dracolysk had died and the laser device had been stolen by a Barney, whom Black Barney had now identified as Sattar Tabibi.

There had been one or two fleeting rumors drifting across the communications channels, which hinted that Kemal had built his bridges at the expense of the people he had originally defended, the Desert Dancers. Huer had dismissed the rumors as space gossip, but now he reconsidered them. Barney's information made his electronic instincts boil. He had, as his friend Buck would have said, a hunch. Something was brewing on Mercury.

"I think I'll pay a visit to Mercury and our friend Kemal," said Huer reflectively.

Barney's small eyes opened in surprise. Any breach of Mercurian security was difficult, whether it meant running a ship through the planet's defenses or leapfrogging a computer lock.

Huer enjoyed the grudging respect his words forced from the pirate. "I've done it before," the digital personality said.

"Mmm."

"One more thing."

Barney looked weary. He had already expended more mental energy than was his wont. He had made an independent decision that was not directly tied to assault, mayhem, or spoil.

"Stay in contact. I may need you," said Huer. His tone was distant, his eyes blank. They were large and brown, and when he was accessing information, they tended to lose expression.

Barney waved the hologram off. He was bored with the conversation. He had not enjoyed Tabibi's boasts and taunts, and he was thinking it would be amusing to disrupt his clone brother's pleasures with a little healthy mayhem.

Huer's eyes focused. He leveled them at the pirate. "You were right to report this," he said. "And I think the captain would agree with me when I ask you not to discuss the subject, especially not outside this ship."

"Um." Barney's acknowledgement was absent. He was considering suitable methods to punish Tabibi.

Konii watched the interchange slyly. Huer was not aware of his presence. The *Free Enterprise*'s holographic eye had a limited range, and Konii was seated outside it. He found the information Barney had passed on interesting, and he was considering ways to use it when his captain caught his eye.

The murderous intent in Barney's eyes pinned Konii to his station like a bug to a card. He did not say a word. He did not have to. Konii knew the implications in those eyes. He swallowed hard, raising one hand in a pledge. Barney nodded shortly and released him.

"Keep this frequency open," said Huer. "And, Barney, if you have nothing better to do, I would appreciate it if you did not stray too far from Mercury."

Barney did not reply. He owed Buck Rogers allegiance because Rogers had fought him and won. He respected Huer because he was Rogers's representative. Barney would report to Huer, but he would not let a digital personality run his ship. If it suited him, he would remain near Mercury. For now, Tortuga suited him.

Huer cleared his throat, aware of the futility of his request but knowing Barney would keep the communications link clear. "Buck will be pleased at your foresight," he said, throwing the faithful hound a bone.

"Cap'n'll blow off steam cruisin' the system," said Barney, referring to Project Deepspace, the mission in which Rogers was now involved.

"Um. Yes." Huer never quite knew how to react to Barney's earthier comments. "I shall refer your good wishes. Should any new information come to light, I would be most interested. I would also be interested in rumors from Mercury."

Barney nodded. "I'll ask the crew," he said. "They got anything, I'll send it."

"Good. If there is nothing else, I will terminate the transmission."

"Affirmative," replied Barney, privately thinking Huer long-winded.

"Huer out," said the hologram as it winked out of existence.

"He seemed unduly interested in the loss of a piece of space junk," commented Konii caustically. His thin face wore a perennially superior expression. His privileged heritage had soured his outlook.

"Expensive junk," said Barney. He glared at Konii once more. "You let the Doc do the thinkin'," he said. "It's his business. Yours is to forget what you heard."

"Of course," said Konii smoothly.

"Mmm," Barney murmured. He did not for a moment believe his officer. There was only one characteristic in Konii's makeup that Barney knew he could rely upon: The man was totally untrustworthy, controlled only by force. Barney showed some now. He was across the bridge in one swift step, one hand clamped around Konii's throat. A foot-long knife flashed out of Barney's wrist, grazing Konii's jaw-bone and drawing blood. "I said it once. I'll not say it again. Stow it."

Konii's eyes nearly popped out of his head and he gurgled wildly. A grim smile played over Barney's mouth, and he dropped the man into his chair like a rag doll.

Chapter Six

Kemal Gavilan paced the security computer
room on Mercury Prime. His uncle Gordon
and cousin Dalton were overseeing the construction of their pet project. Gordon had not invited
Kemal to attend the festivities. This did not surprise
Kemal. His uncle had shown him the laser's plans,
but its location remained a secret. If the project were
a giant edition of the Sun Flower laser he had seen on
Rising Sun, as he had heard Gordon intimate, then
his uncle was wise to keep its whereabouts secure.

From the few sentences he had managed to over-
hear, Kemal deduced that the laser was being constructed on a mammoth scale, its purpose not

asteroid mining, as the computer reports on the project indicated, but widespread destruction. Gordon Gavilan, fresh from defeat by the ragtag forces of Earth-based NEO, was building a super weapon.

Kemal had earned Gordon's respect when he bargained his way into leadership of the laser project on Rising Sun, displacing his cousin Dalton. The loss of the prototype laser had reinforced Gordon's native paranoia, and he was again keeping Kemal at arm's length, though with a difference. Gordon had left him to baby-sit Mercury Prime's complex computer network. Kemal was a family member seated like a flywheel in the center of computer activity, his authorization necessary for all priority-red-coded transmissions; in the complex political structure of Mercury, where espionage was a way of life, such communications were not rare. A highly trained team of computer technicians maintained and monitored Mercury Prime's functions, but Kemal was a backup, and all classified data was fed directly into his hands. He checked the security memory folders every four hours.

Kemal slid down in a chair until he was almost reclining and linked his fingers together across his hard stomach. The computer's blinking lights were a pleasant rainbow in the distance.

The communications chief interrupted the prince's reverie. "Sir, transmission code red four," he said. "Specifically coded for you." The communications chief looked puzzled.

Kemal's fine brows drew together in a frown. "Run it into the box," he said, referring to the luxurious chamber off the computer network that was reserved for Gavilan use. The chamber blocked out the many computer noises as well as human sounds.

Kemal touched a control panel on the wall, and a communications link opened. There was a burst of static as the security sequence went into effect. Once the line was locked in, not even the communications chief could breach it.

"Kemal Gavilan, this is—"

"Doc?" Kemal was incredulous. The voice on the line was a near-impossible falsetto, but he recognized it immediately.

". . . um, yes. Is this a clear line?"

"As clear as they come," answered Kemal. "You're taking a big chance, Doctor Huer. There is no love lost between Mercury and NEO."

"I know it." Huer sounded peeved. His head and shoulders materialized on a computer screen. "Do you think I'm a fool? Do you think I'd risk this if it weren't necessary?"

Kemal grinned at Huer's irascibility. "No," he replied.

"All right, then. I have some information for you."

"Information?" asked Kemal.

"Yes. I've been in contact with Black Barney."

"What?" asked Kemal, all attention.

"According to Barney, the laser prototype was stolen by Sattar Tabibi and sold to Ardala Valmar for a healthy profit."

"So that's who took it. And killed Dracolysk." Kemal mulled Huer's information. "Ardala Valmar."

"Yes."

"Then the laser is still in dangerous hands. Ardala is a viper." Kemal's fine hazel eyes were worried in his bronze face. He ran a hand through his clipped brown hair. "And there's more trouble. Gordon's in the process of building a larger version. As yet, I don't know where."

"Oh. He doesn't trust you?"

Huer's question reminded Kemal of the trust he had thrown away and of the horror in Duernie's eyes at his betrayal. The memory was a knot of pain in his stomach.

"No. He doesn't trust me, in spite of the position I've been forced to take with the Dancers."

"We heard the rumors of your betrayal," said Huer, his voice carefully neutral.

"Yes." Kemal's answer was bleak. "I was forced to. I was followed. They have my complete sympathies, and I will find a way to safeguard them, but, at the moment, I am powerless."

"There are those within NEO who question your loyalties because of it."

"I know. I was on the verge of leaving Mercury. I want the position of Gordon's new laser. If it lives up to the rumors, it would be a doomsday weapon capable of destroying entire cities—possibly states. But I couldn't bring NEO a hypothesis. I had to have proof."

Huer was silent. His circuits were clicking with activity as he pondered Kemal's words. Experience gave him no reason to suspect Kemal. Aside from his recent treatment of the Dancers, his actions within NEO had been exemplary. Huer wished he could discuss the matter with his mentor, Buck Rogers, but in Rogers's absence he made a decision. "Stay on Mercury," he said.

"What?"

"I said, stay on Mercury. You are in a position to do more good than anyone."

"And the new laser?"

"I am afraid you will have to destroy it," said Huer.

Chapter Seven

Kemal's lips twisted in wry humor. The digital personality's assessment of the data might be accurate, but Huer did not always have a firm grasp of the difficulties his solutions presented. "Destroy it."

"Yes." Huer's tone was positive.

"Do you have any idea how?" asked Kemal.

"Not at the present time."

"Do you even," Kemal continued, "know where the laser is located?" Kemal did not wait for Huer's reply. "I thought not. What makes you think my uncle is going to share that knowledge with me?"

"You are of the same blood," said Huer primly. "You

have a better chance than anyone else."

"That's not saying much. I can't pull something like that off alone, and any allies I had on Mercury are gone." Duernie's severe brown face came to mind, sending a hollow pang through his bones.

"You may have to," replied Huer. "I will try to maintain contact, but it will not be easy. Neither Buck nor Wilma are available—as you well know. At the moment, NEO commanders regard you as a free agent. They will be pleased if you further their efforts for peace, but they will not invade Mercurian borders to help you." Huer pulled a pipe from the pocket of his immaculate navy suit and sucked on the stem.

"Friends," said Kemal sourly. "My esteemed uncle has made me a traitor. In the public eye, he holds me close to his breast. Privately, he trusts me no more than a sand adder. Oh, yes, Gordon has placed me in an enviable position."

"Perhaps," said Huer thoughtfully, "for what you must accomplish, he has done you a favor. He cannot now forbid you access to any but his most private quarters. The more you profess sympathy, the more you will disarm him, if not in actual fact, then in action. He will be forced to play out his own hand, to treat you as a member of the family."

"Members of this family have been known to be assassinated," hissed Kemal. "Like my father."

"Ossip?" Huer considered the possibility. He gazed into the empty bowl of his pipe, the fringe of gray hair over his ears a comical accent to his otherwise dapper appearance. "The records do indicate rumors of foul play, but they were never substantiated."

"No more than the reports of my own death will be." Kemal's cryptic comment was laced with bitterness. The anger in his hazel eyes was deep, rising from the depths of childhood to the ghostly visitation that had confirmed his father's murder. The hologram of his dead father rose into his mind's eye, demanding vengeance.

"I do not understand." Huer was genuinely puzzled. "You fought against your family, your home planet, for the salvation of Earth. Now you have a chance to accomplish the same thing for the entire solar system, and you shrink from the task."

"This time I am alone." Kemal roamed the luxurious room, his feet silent on the thick carpeting. "There are no companions to hearten the way, and those I will most probably die for are statistics to me. And I have my father's murderer to catch."

"Kemal, circumstances have placed you here. You are the only one in a position to foil your uncle's plans. A laser of the magnitude you indicate could destroy whole civilizations. There is a delicate balance of life. Civilization—real civilization, the logic and education that lifts humans from the neolithic—hangs in the balance. The laser may not obliterate all human life, but it is capable of pushing the bulk of humanity back into the Stone Age. Life as we know it in the twenty-fifth century would be annihilated."

"You do not have to convince me," said Kemal wearily. "I know. I was simply protesting fate. I am tired of its vagaries. As always, I'll do my best."

"That is all anyone can ask. I promise, Kemal, that whatever happens, NEO will know of your actions."

"And until then, it'll brand me a renegade and put

a price on my head."

"Publicly," agreed Huer, amusement flickering in his brown eyes. "It will help your cover. I'll see to it that the amount is not an insult," said Huer cheerfully. "But you must be convincing. You must forsake your rebellious youth for the wealth and power your family has to offer."

"And if I need to contact you?"

"I will be in touch when I can. You have the emergency code?"

"Strike three," confirmed Kemal.

"Good. Don't use it unless you have to. Huer out."

The communications link went dead, leaving Kemal with questions seething through his brain. He made an angry gesture and cleared the communications line, making sure to erase the conversation. He left the cubicle in long strides, his preoccupied manner inhibiting the computer crew from approaching him. He crossed the room without a word.

As the doors of the computer complex closed behind him, Kemal's shoulders slumped. The task that fate and Huer had handed him was overwhelming, but he knew it had to be done. He wandered down the ornate corridor, oblivious to the intricacies of decoration in the fretwork over each doorway.

"K-K-Kemal! Kemal, wait!"

Kemal heard his cousin's light voice and wearily acknowledged it. He was not in the mood for an interview with earnest but helpless Tix. He kept walking.

Unfortunately for Kemal, Tix was taller than he, and his long legs overtook Kemal easily. The youngest of Gordon Gavilan's legitimate children, Tix was sunshine to his brother Dalton's gloom. He was as

tall as Dalton, but not as heavily built, and where
Dalton was dark, he was fair. His hair was white-
blond, and his startled eyes were bright blue. He
looked like a perennially surprised puppy.

"K-K-Kemal, I want to t-t-talk to you!"

Kemal slowed and turned to face Tix. His cousin
was a year younger than he, but to Kemal he seemed
a child. Conventional Gavilan education had been
wasted on Tix. His transparent mind had no aptitude
for the complex games of diplomacy that his family so
enjoyed.

"Yes, Tix?" answered Kemal, trying to keep the
weariness out of his voice.

"Kemal, I want you to intercede with F-F-Father."

"What?" Kemal was truly surprised. "What makes
you think Gordon would listen to me?"

"He respects you." Tix nodded. "Oh, I know he d-d-
does not trust you, but he respects you. If you asked
him t-t-to let me act as his overseer on the laser project, he would listen. If he thought you had f-f-faith in
me . . . he might even view me in a d-d-different
light."

Tix was entirely aware of his father's feelings toward him. He yearned to distinguish himself in Gordon's eyes, but he did not have the temperament or
skills for military conflict.

"And Dalton?" asked Kemal carefully. "What do
you think your brother would say to such a request?"
He studied Tix's perfectly tailored saffron figure.
Gordon Gavilan would never hand a scientific mission over to his son the dreamer, nor would artistic
Tix distinguish himself in such a project. Kemal was
surprised at Tix's request.

Tix shrugged, his embroidered saffron robes shimmering. "N-N-Nothing. He has no interest in anything but war. He wants nothing to do with F-F-Father's project until it can be put into use." He regarded Kemal enviously. "F-F-Father put you in charge of Rising Sun Station over Dalton."

Kemal's mind was circling the issue. Tix's assessment of his brother Dalton was inaccurate. For the first time it occurred to him to wonder exactly how much Tix knew. "Tix, do you really want this?"

Tix hung his head, but he did not answer.

Kemal patted his cousin's arm. He clasped his hands behind his back and continued down the hall, Tix at his side.

"Think of it, K-K-Kemal! A weapon so powerful that n-n-no one would dare risk its use."

"A deterrent," said Kemal heavily. "An interesting piece of psychology. Historically, it has not proved effective."

"What do you mean?" asked Tix.

"I mean, Cousin, that it doesn't work. Sooner or later, angel or madman—someone—decides the circumstances warrant its use. Look at the weapon Buck Rogers destroyed in the twentieth century. Had it remained operational, Anatoly Karkov—a madman if ever there was one—would have used that weapon to destroy millions. Not so many years later, the Last Gasp War turned Earth into a steaming nuclear waste dump because someone could not resist using a weapon."

Kemal shook his head. "So, where is Uncle Gordon constructing this humanitarian device?"

"Oh, he had a special l-l-laboratory built for it. It's

supposed to look like p-p-part of the Mariposas, for security reasons," said Tix.

"Admirable," replied Kemal, privately trying to remember the number of satellites dotting space around the planet.

Tix stretched out a hand and grasped Kemal's arm. "Thanks, Cousin," he said.

"For what?" asked Kemal.

"For l-l-listening to me. I'm no good at war, but I am good with my hands. I'm good at b-b-building things. I want to show Father what I can d-do."

"Tix, you have taste and talent. Why waste your abilities on a mechanical monolith when you could be turning Mercury Prime into beauty?"

"Beauty," answered Tix coldly, "does not impress F-Father."

Kemal watched Tix's back as he walked away. He liked Tix. He was about to use him to get to Gordon's solar laser. He tried to rationalize his actions through the knowledge that his mission would benefit Tix along with everyone else, but to no avail. He felt cheap and dirty.

"Why, Kemal, why so serious? You are not half so handsome when you frown."

Kemal started at the musical words. "Hello, Ramora," he said.

"Is that all you have to say? 'Hello, Remora'? I was hoping for something more personal."

Ramora's voice was like silk. It slid over Kemal's libido, lifting the hairs at the back of his neck. Ramora was his uncle's favorite concubine, a woman in her mid-twenties, old enough to know pleasure, young enough to give it. She had thick brown hair that tum-

bled in an unruly mass of curls around her seductive
face. Her round brown eyes professed supreme inno-
cence. They lied. Her baby face had deceived more
than one man into trusting her. Ramora was a dangerous woman, just coming into her own. Kemal
knew his peril.

"I do not usurp another's rights," said Kemal
lightly.

Ramora pouted. She ran her fingers up his chest
and locked her hands behind his neck, her warm
bosom nestled against him. "Gordon is an old man.
He grows tired."

"Careful, Ramora," cautioned Kemal.

Ramora shook her beautiful head. "I don't care. I
am tired of stories about people I never knew, people
dead before my time."

"Stories?" asked Kemal. "That sounds fascinat-
ing."

"Maybe to you," said Ramora. "You're Gavilan.
You'd like hearing about your ancestors and for-
bears. I like the present," she said.

"Ancestors?" asked Kemal lightly, trying not to
make his inquiry seem important.

"Hundreds of them. Sun Kings and princes and
barons and counts and whatever, until I could
scream. Gordon talks about them all."

"Even . . . my father?" Kemal's concentration was
faltering.

"I don't know," said Ramora, her parted lips hovering a hairsbreadth from his, her eyes closed to curved
slits. "What was his name again?"

"Ossip," said Kemal, breathing the name into her
hair.

A line of concentration appeared between her fine brows. Kemal did not see it. His eyes were blurred with the sight of her exquisite face so close to his. He knew Gordon would kill him if he found her with him, yet at this moment, he did not care. Ramora was intoxicating.

"Ossip," Ramora repeated, making the name a melody. "Yes. Not often."

Kemal fought for control. "I did not know my father," he said. "And I have always been afraid to ask my uncle about him. He does not mention him in my hearing. I would be most grateful for whatever you could remember. Perhaps we should find somewhere comfortable to talk," he suggested.

"Yes," answered Ramora, but she did not unlock her arms.

Through the silk fabric of her long dress, Kemal could feel her heart quicken, feel her warmth. He glanced down the deserted corridor, then reached up and grasped one of her hands, freeing himself. He knew he was under the watchful eye of a surveillance camera. "I welcome your conversation, my lady," he said, placing heavy emphasis on the word 'conversation.'

Ramora chuckled. "No doubt we shall communicate," she replied. "Come! I will tell you all about your father." She turned to the camera and stuck out her tongue.

"I find your actions forward," Kemal said.

Ramora laughed.

Chapter Eight

The five-note melody that was Kemal Gavilan's personal intercom identification code sounded its lilting music in the cozy confines of a sitting room in the Gavilan apartments. Kemal leaned across Ramora's clinging figure and pushed the activator panel set in the wall's woodwork. "This is Kemal," he said.

"I am sorry to disturb you, sir, but Gordon Gavilan is on the line."

"Put my uncle on visual," replied Kemal, and Gordon Gavilan's heavy, handsome face, with its prominent nose and the distinguished frosting of gray in his dark hair, materialized on the screen.

"Well," said Gordon, with a spice of malice in his voice, "I see you are enjoying yourself, Ramora."

Ramora pouted charmingly, playing along with Gordon's pretension of ignorance concerning her presence in Kemal's quarters, but she did not move away from Kemal. "You went away, Gordon. You are always away since you started building that stupid device."

Gordon ignored her. His words were for Kemal. "I expect dedication from family, Kemal."

"And you have had it. Since you did not see fit to include the entire family," Kemal said, putting emphasis on the last word, "on your inspection tour, I am passing the time as best I can. And your precious communications system just cleared my . . . check."

Gordon's eyes were raw with anger. "And so you use that as an excuse to philander away the afternoon?" He sneered.

"On the contrary. I have spent twenty minutes trying to pry information out of your favorite concubine."

Gordon stared at his nephew. Kemal's oval face was bland. In spite of himself, a glimmer of admiration for Kemal's audacity tugged Gordon Gavilan's severe mouth into a twist of a smile. "And were you successful?" he asked dryly.

Kemal shook his head regretfully. "No. She knows nothing of value." In fact, Kemal had picked up several interesting tidbits of information concerning his father.

"Did you actually think me fool enough to trust a woman with anything of importance?"

"Not really," answered Kemal, "but it was worth

the effort." He let his eyes slide sideways appreciatively. Ramora was nibbling up his neck. "Are you returning to Mercury Prime?"

"Within the hour," said Gordon.

"I will be waiting," said Kemal, ignoring Ramora's attentions.

"Ramora, if I catch you in my nephew's quarters again, I'll find more than suitable accommodations for your burning desires—on the sands of Mercury without a lifesuit! Now, get out!" Gordon's furrowed face faded from the screen.

The communications link beeped, followed by the communication chief's voice. "Sir, I have a schooner standing by. She has orders to clear with your uncle."

"Will no one else do?" asked Kemal.

"The captain says his orders specify Gordon Gavilan."

"Then he'll have to wait. Gordon should be returning soon." As an afterthought Kemal asked, "Where is that schooner's home port?"

"She's surface based, registered out of Tir Plantia Warren."

A special shipment. Crystals? Kemal wondered. Perhaps Dancer crystals? Surely, he thought, it must have something to do with Gordon's pet project. Tantalizing bits of information, disconnected and frustrating, floated in his mind. Not the least of them were Ramora's fragments of information about his father, Ossip. Kemal knew, as he knew his own mind, that his father had been murdered but he could not prove it. He could not even state an unequivocal motive, yet he knew his father to be the victim of foul play. He had determined to avenge his father's death.

Gordon's comments to Ramora had been cryptic and unrewarding, interesting only in the jealousy they indicated, a jealousy that had not abated through the years despite Ossip's death. Kemal knew only enough to want to know more.

"Thank you," he finally replied to the patient communication chief. "I shall be on the docks, should you need me." He flipped off the intercom and shrugged out from under Ramora's clinging body.

"You're going, too," she said, letting her hands slide off Kemal.

Kemal regarded her ironically. "Yes. You are a dangerous minx. Uncle Gordon is welcome to you."

Ramora smirked, and on such an exquisite face, it was not unattractive. "We'll see," she said sweetly. "I think you're all bravado, Kemal Gavilan—empty bravado. You will not be able to stay away from me any more than Dalton has been." She laughed.

Kemal filed that piece of information for future reference. As he escaped into the corridor, her laughter was cut off, but it continued to heckle him. He thought of Duernie and her quiet seriousness, so unlike Ramora's blatant advances but just as compelling. The Dancer had trusted him, risked her life for him. She had been a friend, and he had repaid her by throwing her people to the Gavilan wolves.

He tried not to think of her, lest the pain overwhelm him.

O O O O O

Duernie studied the computer screen, her black eyes intense, her strong eyebrows drawn down over

the bridge of her pert nose in her characteristic
frown. Her slim body was bent forward, the loose,
one-piece white gown she wore belted at the waist
with links of brass. In the controlled atmosphere of
her apartment in the track city of Renaissance Gold,
the gown was comfortable.

Space was at a premium in the track cities. She was
fortunate to have her own apartment, earned
through years of hard work negotiating mining con-
tracts for the Dancers. The room was a model of efficiency. Two comfortable red gel chairs, light enough
to be stacked at night, sat in the center of the room.
Dumbwaiter terminals for food delivery were re-
cessed into the walls, a keypunch panel beside them.
Sanitary facilities were hidden behind a frosted
quarter-round panel in one corner of the room. The
touch of a button would lift Duernie's bed from its re-
cessed compartment in the floor. Made, like the
chairs, of flexible gel, it was thin but totally comfortable. Her function as a Dancer representative allowed Duernie a personal computer terminal with
security access, and she used it now.

Across the computer screen glared the most frustrating word she knew: "classified." Her frown deepened, and she cleared the screen, then keyed in a new
access reference. "Scan 'butterfly'," she typed.

The terminal digested her request, then threw a
menu onto the screen. There were six entries. Duernie began to access them. Three of the entries concerned species of insects once indigenous to Old
Earth. She typed in the fourth entry, "butterfly net,"
and was rewarded with another classified code, but
this time she smiled. The expression gave considera-

ble charm to her severe face. After the classified code was the number four. She held a security four clearance, so she accessed the file.

A slow whistle escaped her as the screen scrolled a series of structural readouts. She stopped the scroll, grinning at the notation on the bottom of the screen, the white light from the computer terminal washing out the bronze color of her skin. "Mariposa Solar Energy Satellite XXVII," said the label.

She had finally managed to find the technical readouts of the Gavilans' precious Mariposas. Of course, these were old scans, and they would not contain surveillance and security systems, but it was a start. It was definitely a start. She had plans for the Mariposas.

Duernie's anger had hardened into resolve. She intended to hurt the Gavilans as Kemal Gavilan had hurt her. He valued the money that the crystals could bring more than honor—more than friendship? Then she would make him pay in a coin he understood: money.

She scrolled the computer screen back to the start of the file and began to study the readouts.

○ ○ ○ ○ ○

Kemal slumped into a chair in the control room of Mercury Prime's main docking bay, waiting for his uncle's return. The room was paneled with computer screens, one screen for each mooring, and several extra to handle an overview of the entire area. The docks were busy, for Mercury Prime did a brisk trade with other planets as well as the Mercurian surface warrens and Dancer track cities. Mercury Prime specialized in zero gravity manufacture. The station's ample power supplies made this a profitable business sidelight for the Gavilans.

Technicians manned the monitors around him. Kemal could hear one man talking to the navigator on his uncle's ship. Kemal stretched out his long legs and waited; the chirping of the computer terminals was soothing.

"Kemal."

Kemal started. The voice was barely audible, but he recognized it immediately. It was his father's voice. He glanced furtively around the room, but the technicians were involved with their work.

"Kemal." The whisper sounded again.

"Yes," replied Kemal, his voice low, his face wary.

"Do not trust Ramora."

"I don't," Kemal answered. He searched the computer screens around him, but they all were either focused on the docks or blank. The hologram of his father, which Kemal had first discovered in his private chambers, was nowhere to be found.

"Gordon uses his girls as spies, trains them for it," continued the whisper. "When they know too much, they disappear." One of the blank screens shimmered with the words.

"Could she know enough to help me?" Kemal murmured.

"Gordon plays close to his chest," said Ossip. "He will trust no one. You must make him betray what he knows."

"How?" said Kemal. Both Huer and his father seemed to be asking the impossible of him.

Ossip's voice sighed. "If I knew that, Kemal, I could have solved my own murder long ago."

There was a subtle change in the sound, and Kemal knew the digital twin that his father had programmed into Mercury Prime's computer system had ceased transmission.

"You all right?" came another voice.

Kemal jerked, startled by the computer technician standing behind him.

The man smiled at him. "You look like you've heard the ghost in the machine." He chuckled. "Don't worry, it's a friendly haunt."

Chapter Nine

Gordon Gavilan surveyed the docks coldly. Mercury was a small planet in the sunward crossing. Its strategic location and low gravity made it a superb military base. He did not intend that base to fall into the hands of other powers. The crystal shipment he had been expecting lay safely at anchor, ready for transport to the Mariposa laboratory. The knowledge was a notch on the side of security. He turned to his son Dalton, who stood silently by his left shoulder. "Authorize transport," he said. "Security one."

Dalton nodded, silent.

"I want the prototype back," said Gordon evenly,

"before it falls into other hands."

"Perhaps I have an answer for that," said Kemal softly. He leaned against the hatch to the control center.

Dalton sent him a dark look, but Gordon whirled on his nephew.

"Keeping something from me?" the big man snarled. "You ought to know by now, that is not wise."

"No. I simply have not had an opportunity to explain. There are pirates on Tortuga."

"There are always pirates on Tortuga," snapped Gordon.

Kemal nodded. "These were talking."

"Where did you get this information?" asked Dalton, suspicious. His broad shoulders squared under his elaborately embroidered black shirt.

Kemal's hazel eyes glittered with sparks of anger. "I have my sources," he replied. "Believe me, they are reliable."

Dalton looked unconvinced.

"So far, I have heard nothing." Gordon advanced a step, but Kemal remained relaxed against the door frame.

"If my esteemed cousin would let me talk, I might be able to tell you something. It seems a notorious pirate, one Sattar Tabibi, was boasting to his compatriots about his theft from the Gavilans. He let slip that he had sold the device to Ardala Valmar."

"Valmar! The plans, not to say the laser, are long gone!" groused Dalton.

"Perhaps not," replied Kemal. "Ardala likes money. She may be willing to return the laser for a price."

"More than she could sell it for on the open market," agreed Dalton.

"No price is too high." Gordon's cold fury burned in his eyes, like fanatical flashes of rage.

Dalton watched his father's flaring anger out of the corner of his eye. Gordon's violent mood swings were not the signs of a stable mind.

"I might be able to contact her." Kemal made his offer soft. Not long ago, his uncle Gordon had referred to the prototype as a toy, its loss hardly worthy of his notice.

Gordon advanced on his nephew until he loomed over him, his eyes boring into Kemal's face.

Kemal dropped his disinterested pretense and stood straight, his athletic body on the defensive. "Don't you think I want that lens back, too? Whatever you may think, I am a Gavilan. That device was taken from *us*. No one has that right."

These were words Gordon wanted to hear, and Kemal's eyes, so like his father's, made Gordon want to trust him. Far at the back of the Sun King's mind was a feathery voice that said Kemal was an unreliable. Gordon decided to overrule it.

"All right. You have my authorization. Go to Ardala. Offer her whatever it takes. The return of the laser is paramount."

Kemal's eyes glinted with sardonic humor, but his mouth was grim. He made a short salute and turned on his heel. Gordon watched him go down the corridor, curiously pleased by Kemal's immediate response and the clipped efficiency of his stride.

"Father!" Dalton's voice was a whisper of disbelief. "I cannot believe you are trusting that whelp on a mission of such importance!"

"Would you have me send you?" Gordon shook his head. "I think Kemal will accomplish his task. Besides, he is unknown to Ardala. She likes adventure. And, my son, I think it would be much better if you were to follow him."

Dalton's tense shoulders relaxed. "I do not trust him," he acknowledged.

Dalton remembered his first sight of his cousin after years of separation. Kemal had struck him as small. Dalton was a broad man, thick of bone and muscle. He saw Kemal's wiry strength as weakness, and the impression had never left him. In spite of Kemal's achievements in the Martian Wars, in spite of his facility with a knife and the quickness that could kill in hand-to-hand combat before most men could move, Dalton clung to his emotional reaction. Grudgingly, he accorded Kemal respect, but he cherished the illusion that Kemal was his inferior, as well as a political rival he did not want.

"A natural competition between young men." Gordon grinned.

"No," said Dalton. "More. Since his return from the Martian Wars, he has been remarkably Mercurian—even though he fought against us for the cause of NEO. He admits that that renegade, Rogers, is his friend."

"Is it not possible he has seen the error of his ways?" asked Gordon. "He proved his fealty to us on Rising Sun."

Dalton's brooding face went grim. "He fought with us," he admitted.

"With NEO he has nothing: a blasted planet that

will take a century to rebuild, no home, no ties, merely questionable friends," said Gordon. "Perhaps he sees the advantage of his ancestral home, where we live in luxury and absolute power."

Dalton considered his father's words, but his dark expression did not lift. "No," the younger man said finally. "I cannot believe it." He raised his eyes to his father's. "I accept the possibility, but I cannot believe it."

"Then," said Gordon, "this will be another good test. If Kemal accomplishes his purpose and returns the solar laser to us, we will have greater reason to believe a change of heart. If not, we will know."

Dalton nodded, his heavy mane of black hair shining blue under the ship's lights.

○ ○ ○ ○ ○

Ardala Valmar's fairy-tale castle sat on a hill outside the sprawling Martian city of Coprates Metroplex. One of her many residences, it commanded the surrounding countryside. From the highest turret, she could see the apex of the Metroplex itself, a streamlined pyramid rising into the clear Martian sky. It was not a sight she often sought.

Ardala was a hot-house plant, not a creature of the open air. She preferred to spend her time within the luxurious confines of her home. Her wealth had made it a tribute to her whims, from the pale pink marble flagstones of the main hall, to the rich wood-paneled interior of her study. The study was her favorite room, an office that doubled as recreation area, for Ardala's passion was making money.

Behind her elaborately carved desk, she indulged
herself, seeking profit from the merest hints and intimations. An entire wall of the study was devoted to a
computer-communications screen, which ran a con-
tinuous roll of data twenty-four and a half hours a
day.

The computer communicated visually. Ardala dis-
liked conversation with machines, and she never allowed herself to be contradicted. Her computer was
linked to the main Martian communications channels and, through them, to outposts all over the solar
system. Moreover, Ardala had her own money-
making interests scattered over the system, each one
of which had a direct line to her home base. She was
not so much an investor as an information broker.
Her wares required no warehouse space and cost only
the price of a com-line to transport. Her own diversi-
fied interests included a series of casinos and mining
claims in the belt, silent partnerships in several
multimillion-credit Martian businesses, a line of
ships, and numerous interests in free space stations.
From these investments, her personal intelligence
network informed her of unusual activity in their areas. In the line of business, she cultivated dangerous
acquaintances.

It had been no surprise when Sattar Tabibi contacted her with contraband to sell. Ardala's broker-
age was ninety percent legitimate, but some of her
best profit margins came from deals she struck under
the table. Tabibi's hot laser was one of them. The moment he told her of his coup against the Gavilans and
the nature of his haul, she had been interested. She
had immediately seen two possible avenues of profit.

The Gavilans might be lured into ransoming their invention, or a certain mining magnate she knew in the belt would pay dearly for such a potentially efficient asteroid carver. The military possibilities of the lens were a more delicate matter.

She had bought the lens from Tabibi and immediately set her own scientific staff to work on it, intending to produce a complete set of blueprints and technical readouts for sale, as well as the prototype. She expected it to be a profitable investment.

Ardala leaned back in her deeply upholstered red leather chair, her head tilted back over the curving top. A relative of the Martian royal family, Ardala had been reared to wealth. She looked it. From the top of her glossy black head to the tips of her manicured toes, she radiated care. Her black hair was perfectly cut, thick and shiny against the red chair. Her tilted, dark eyes, languid as she considered her possible dealings with the Gavilans, were perfectly shadowed, the thick, curling lashes judiciously augmented with mascara. Her voluptuous mouth was tinted baby pink, making it a kissable rosebud. She wore a white leather jumpsuit like a second skin. It was shiny where her curves filled it out, and the deep V-neck revealed her full bosom. She had slipped her white sandals off and had pulled her long legs into the chair, curling up like a cat.

The Gavilans were indeed her first line of attack. They were rich—richer than she was, and that was no mean feat. She ran over the prominent names in her mind. Gordon Gavilan, leader of the pack, ruler of Mercury, was a man who had come to prominence through his military acumen. Unlike many of his predecessors, he had a reputation for ruthlessness and the most exciting mouth she knew.

Ossip was dead, of course, and Gordon's other brother, Garrick, had been absent so long that everyone assumed he had died as well.

Dalton Gavilan, young, ambitious, heartless, was a younger physical approximation of his father, though he had a heaviness that repelled her. Though fit, his solid bone structure gave an impression of weight. He would be the next ruler of Mercury.

There was Tix, too, though the simpleton was hardly worth considering.

Then there was the renegade, a renegade who had returned to the arms of his family. Kemal Gavilan did not have the dramatic looks of his uncle and cousin, yet the few pictures she had of Kemal interested her. For one thing, he was young, full of passion and fire. Ardala could see it in the carriage of his head and the set of his shoulders. He had flown in the face of powerful relatives to aid his friends with NEO, and that rebelliousness attracted her.

She ran the tip of her pink tongue over her generous lips. She would not mind tasting Gavilan coffers. She smiled, and her eyes closed like a cat's.

"Your pardon, my lady."

"What is it, Raj? I told you I did not wish to be disturbed." The annoyance in her voice was the petulance of a spoiled child.

Raj sank under it. He prostrated himself at her feet, one hand extended. In it he clutched a fold of paper. "A pirate delivered this moments ago. He would not stay, but he said Redbeard sent it, and that you must see it immediately."

Ardala tweaked the piece of paper from the pleasure gennie's hands, leaving him humbled before her. She unfolded it and read the contents, then tossed the paper onto her desk. "Well," she said. "It seems I should not have been angry with you." Her voice, a moment ago laced with anger, was as smooth as honey.

Raj raised his head, his eyes pleading like a spaniel's. Ardala reached out a perfect hand and ran one pink fingernail along his throat. Raj swallowed and closed his eyes.

"It was useful information, Raj," she said caressingly. "You must be rewarded for your service. Now, what, I wonder, would you like?" Her slow smile was full of promise.

"Whatever is your pleasure, my lady," he replied, his words slow because of the effort it took to form them. He trembled under her touch.

Information was Ardala's passion, but passion was her hobby. Men were her slaves, in heart as well as body, and though she ruled them with cruel whimsy, most of them would have died for her. Raj was one of them.

Ardala leaned forward until her breast hovered over him. "Send a message to Redbeard with the next ship. I will provide a secure channel when he wishes to contact me. Tell him to use the code word 'booty'."

"Yes, my lady," whispered Raj.

Ardala let her full lips sink against his, then kissed him with a courtesan's accomplishment. She could feel him shaking. She broke the kiss and smiled at him, her cat's eyes inscrutable. Her pleasure gennies knew the rules. She could do as she pleased to them,

but they were not to touch her unless invited. "Draw
me a bath, Raj. Perhaps I will allow you to scrub my
back."

The hope that flared in his eyes was pathetic, and
Ardala enjoyed it. She waved him off, and Raj
crawled backward, not rising until he had reached
the door to her study.

"I want confirmation on that message," she said.

"Of course, my lady. I will find a messenger at once.
Your bath will be ready in five minutes."

Ardala watched his respectful retreat. Her gennies
were tailored to her tastes, physically varied and
emotionally identical. For the most part, they satisfied her. Occasionally, however, she found herself
bored. Kemal's handsome young face teased the
edges of her mind.

Chapter Ten

Duernie paced the confines of her room on Renaissance Gold. The track city's continual vibration did not impede her stride. She had studied the Mariposas until their specifications were part of her. The more she knew of them, the more awesome she found them to be. She had always known, intellectually, their value. Now she understood. They provided wealth that should be used to ease the lives of all on Mercury, not feather the Gavilan's nest of Mercury Prime. They kept the surface dwellers in financial slavery. There were hollows, but she could not sleep. With the Gavilans in orbit around it, the surface would never be free.

What frightened Duernie most was her desire for destruction. She longed to eliminate the Mariposas, and, in her careful study of their construction, she had found a way to do it. This was a temptation of the soul, a chance to wreak havoc on a man she had trusted and who had betrayed that trust. The thought of breaking Kemal, of reducing his proud Gavilan carriage to a shambles of poverty and loss, was seduction itself.

Kemal's handsome face, with laughter hovering at the corners of his golden eyes, mocked her. She railed at herself for having trusted any man, much less a Gavilan. Long ago, another man had taught her the futility of trusting love. It was a lesson she learned well, locking herself away from involvement, making her liaisons physical and fleeting. She had managed with that, preferring emptiness to pain, until Kemal.

He had not asked for her love or demanded her body. He had treated her with respect. That, from a Gavilan, was a miracle. As she had come to know him better, Duernie realized Kemal had been raised a military man, not a political schemer, though his mind was quick. She doubted that many of his family's manipulations would go unnoticed. As she and he had been thrown together, they had become friends, comfortable with one another, learning to trust each other as circumstances proved the worth of each.

The memories brought tears to her eyes. They stung. She wiped them away with a brown hand. Duernie prided herself on facing the unvarnished truth. She faced it now, squarely. Her anger at Kemal was real. She felt betrayed. But what she wanted most of all was to find her knowledge false, to find that he was still her friend, still cared for her, still supported her people. In spite of circumstances, in spite of appearances, her heart ached to hear its desires confirmed.

She loved him. That was the basic truth she had to face. For good or ill, she was tied to Kemal, whether she reacted against him or supported him. She remembered the feel of his arm around her and trembled with desire. No other man had ever awakened such feeling. Duernie knew she could not turn away from Kemal until she knew he no longer cared.

Now, here on Mercury, she could not reach him, but perhaps she could reach his friend, Huer. Once the quixotic digital personality had demanded her help to save Kemal. Now she would ask him for the same.

With Duernie, thought was action. She picked up a short cloak and threw it around her shoulders, locked the door of her room, and headed for the skimmer docks with long strides. Her face was taut with purpose, and the few people she passed at this late hour left her strictly alone. The communications link in her room was not secure. The one in her skimmer was.

She reached the docks, handed the steward her boarding pass, and he opened the security gate. At the end of the docks was her craft, snugged to its mooring. She unlocked it, freed the line, and climbed in. The skimmer bounced under her weight. With the push of a button, the engine roared to life. She let it idle a few moments to warm up, for the skimmer was old and crotchety, then backed slowly away from the dock. The maneuver took some skill, for all the while the track city was rolling over the desert.

Once free, she turned her craft and sent it flowing over the ground into the darkness, her infrared viewscreen showing her the rough terrain. Twenty miles in the distance she could see a rise, the worn edge of an old crater. She made for it, running without lights, away from Renaissance Gold. She sent her craft up the long incline, then turned it along the rim of the crater, cut the engine, and pulled up the communications system.

A short numerical code scrambled the messages. She checked for a communication satellite, located the nearest, and set the directional system for its coordinates. A blue light came on under the keypad, indicating that she had a link with solar lines off Mercury. She keyed in a sequence Huer had once given her, hoping, even if it had been deactivated, that he would recognize it. The sequence went out over the communications lines, and she waited five minutes, then keyed it again. The backup sent, she settled into her seat to wait. She had barely closed her eyes when a strident beep interrupted her relaxation.

"This is Duernie," she said into the link. "Come in."

"Confirm," said a familiar voice at the end of the link.

"How am I supposed to do that?" she asked. "You asked me to take you on faith. You're going to have to do the same."

The link beeped again, and the system's small holographic eye activated. Huer popped into existence beside her, sitting catty-corner on the skimmer's passenger seat. "We meet again," he said, his fine eyebrows lifting over expressive brown eyes.

"Yes." Duernie regarded Huer suspiciously. "Your response was quick. I did not expect you to be able to circumvent Gavilan security so quickly."

Huer smiled. "Since our last problem with the esteemed Gavilans, I thought it prudent to prepare a more accessible doorway."

Duernie said nothing.

"You wished to speak with me?" prompted Huer.

"I thought so, when I contacted you. Now I am not so sure."

"Why?" asked Huer innocently.

"Because I am not sure I can trust you. You are Kemal's friend."

"As are you," responded Huer.

Duernie shook her head slowly, sadly. "No. I cannot be. He has betrayed me. He has betrayed the Dancers." This time, Huer did not reply. Duernie was quick to note his reticence.

"I find this difficult to accept," she said. The words were not easy.

"And you contacted me."

"Yes."

"Why not ask Kemal about his motives?" said Huer.

"I no longer have free access to him. He is a Gavilan, and Gavilans do not mix with Dancers, especially if they have betrayed them. The Dancers would kill him."

"And you?"

"I might as well. I do not know. But, for the sake of

what I thought was friendship, I had to try to find out more. I do not want to believe the truth. I do not wish to believe Kemal Gavilan is not my friend."

"Kemal's position here on Mercury is difficult. You, of all people, should appreciate that. He walks a fine line with his family. His part in the Martian Wars did not inspire their trust."

"I thought he did not care for them," said Duernie bleakly. "I thought he cared for his friends in the resistance, for Rogers and Deering, and for you."

"He cares for us," said Huer. His circuits were buzzing as he tried to sort what he could and could not safely tell Duernie. He did not dare trust her entirely.

"I thought he cared for me." The words were bitter and vulnerable. They were out before Duernie thought, and she regretted them.

Huer looked her full in the face. He studied the severe contours, softened now by sadness. His programming was set to relieve human suffering, and he wished to ease her hurt, but he could not trust Kemal's security to her. He hedged.

"Duernie, if there is one thing I have learned from humans, it is that in certain circumstances the heart is the only guide. It is sometimes truer than all the logic I can muster. I cannot tell you what is inside Kemal's heart. I do not know. I know the circumstances and the appearances. No doubt, you know them as well as I. You must make the choice, for good or ill. You must be ruled by your heart or your head. I cannot give you more."

"Then he is not working for NEO." The grimness was back in her voice.

"The NEO council has no comment on his recent

actions," replied Huer, stating facts.

"And his friends? Rogers, who sent you to save his life?"

Duernie was treading on dangerous ground. Huer replied again with facts. "Rogers has left Kemal to his own devices," he said.

A flash of black pain tore through Duernie's eyes. "Even you do not trust him! Why do you protect him? Why not call him what he is? A traitor and a thief of trust."

"Kemal Gavilan," said Huer, "is a man of intelligence and skill. That is what I know for certain."

"It is not enough," said Duernie coldly.

"That," replied Huer, "is your decision."

Duernie turned away from him, her gaze on the bleak Mercurian landscape. She was a child of this planet, reared on its stark plains. She loved it. Kemal, for all his name and rank, was an outsider. He could never understand. She had been a fool to think he might.

O O O O O

Ardala's computer screen blipped. The hesitation caught her attention. It was followed by a momentary blankness, then the word "booty" appeared, a letter at a time, across its blue surface. The white characters sparkled, and Ardala smiled at them. She hit the voice access.

"Security line confirmed," she said. "You are free to speak."

The screen broke up, and a face she had recently considered appeared on it. Kemal Gavilan, dressed in a fitted shirt decorated with gold piping that followed the trim lines of his torso and accentuated the width of his shoulders, smiled at her. He used all the charm at his disposal in that smile, knowing Ardala's tastes. Though she did not let it stand in the way of business, she was not immune to an attractive man. "Miss Valmar," Kemal acknowledged.

Ardala inclined her lovely head. Today she was dressed in green, her mouth coral, her eyes painted to resemble a butterfly wing, pink shading to iridescent green. She was dramatic against the red leather chair, her dress falling off one creamy shoulder. Kemal noticed all this, noticed her voluptuous curves straining against the fabric, and steeled himself to ignore it. He had not come face-to-face with Ardala before, and the experience was unforgettable. She was one of those women born to drive men wild.

"You wish to speak to me?" she asked negligently.

"Yes." Kemal decided to drive for the heart. "I believe you have something that belongs to my family."

Ardala shook her head. It made her shoulder-length hair a cloud of black around her face. "Impossible. What I have is mine."

"Perhaps if I put in another way . . . You have recently come into possession of a laser."

"Oh, that." Ardala feigned indifference.

"Yes. That. It was stolen from us—though I am sure you have no knowledge of the theft. We would like to have it back."

"As you said, I have no knowledge of illegal actions. As far as I can see, the laser is mine. I will make a comfortable profit on it."

"The Gavilans would not cheat you of a profit you

justly deserve," said Kemal smoothly, running his eyes slowly down her neck. He watched Ardala preen under the tribute, and had to break it to retain control of his voice. "We are prepared to pay handsomely for its return."

"I am interested in making a profit, nothing more," said Ardala.

"As I said, we are willing to pay."

"I require a cash deposit to hold your lens."

Kemal shook his head. "We require that the entire transaction be circumspect. We will bring payment in full to a rendezvous point, and . . ." Kemal let the word hang in the air. ". . . we will deal only with you. No underlings, no computerized transfers. You name the rendezvous."

Ardala's tilted eyes snapped. She did not like ultimatums, yet she was roused by Kemal's audacity. "Tortuga," she replied coldly. "And come alone. I will deal with no one but you. Be prepared to pay two million credits. Cash. Make sure they are unmarked—believe me, I will know the difference. That will be your down payment."

"That should be quite enough," said Kemal.

"Perhaps. In money. There are other kinds of payment."

Kemal's smile flared again. "Believe me, Miss Valmar, any supplemental payment you wish to exact will be my pleasure."

"See you remember that," said Ardala. "Twenty-four hours. There is a private villa off the far side of the station. You will be there."

"At your convenience, my lady," said Kemal.

"Yes," said Ardala.

Chapter Eleven

Kemal paced the anteroom of his apartments on Mercury Prime. The accommodations were plush, all overstuffed velvet and deep carpets and intricate metalwork. With its rose, white, and gold motif, it was an appropriate setting for an houri, but not for a military man. Kemal felt stifled in it, but he knew the rooms to be secure. He had gone over them himself and had enlisted Huer's expertise as well. Only in these few rooms, on all of Mercury Prime, was he free to speak and act as he would, for he had installed his own electronic safeguards against intrusion.

His interview with Ardala loomed over him like a

sentence. He had not realized that she would be so devastatingly beautiful. She had the kind of physical attractiveness that made a man forget how to speak. He needed solid ammunition for his interview, and all he had was Gordon's financial carte blanche. He knew it would not be enough.

"Kemal." The honeyed feminine voice lost none of its cloying sweetness over the intercom.

Kemal opened the door, revealing Ramora, clad in filmy pink. The form-fitting gown left nothing to the imagination. Seductive as a kitten, she sidled up to him.

"And how is my esteemed uncle?" asked Kemal.

Ramora pouted. "How would I know? All he has time for is his silly laser. I thought we might talk some more . . . about your father."

Kemal regarded her sardonically. Her interest in him was dangerous. However, she was privy to Gordon's intimate life, and that could be useful. She stretched out on a convenient love seat, displaying her charms to her best advantage.

"So you have come to me to make him jealous," said Kemal, pouring a glass of orange liquid. She had no way of knowing it was fruit juice. He sipped slowly.

"Yes."

Kemal's eyes twinkled. "You are honest. Gordon is a fool to ignore you."

"I think so, too. He spends all his time with that silly laser, and it's not even completed!"

"The least he could do is include you in his trips," the prince ventured.

Ramora pouted. "Who wants to go to a boring old laboratory? There's not even any gravity."

So, thought Kemal, the laser was being constructed in zero gravity. That meant space. There were no new satellites in orbit, so the laboratory must be located on an existing structure.

"Why would I want to go to a solar collector? I like it here better." She reached out to Kemal. "Come and sit down, so we can talk."

Solar collector. A Mariposa. It made sense. The satellite would provide an immediate power source for any equipment used in constructing the laser. Kemal took another sip of juice. "I don't think talk is your intention," he said dryly. "And I have a healthy respect for my uncle's property."

"Coward!" said Ramora, her full mouth disappointed.

"Definitely," replied Kemal, "especially where my uncle's temper is concerned."

"He said your father was a fool and a wastrel!" she blurted, intent on hurting him.

"Did he, now? Those qualities would make Father a considerable liability." Kemal's tone was mild.

"He also said Ossip was a trusting incompetent who was ruled by his heart."

"So I have heard," replied Kemal. He swirled the juice around in the goblet, knowing his indifference would spur Ramora to weightier insults.

"He said," Ramora offered with a sneer, "that he was not fit to rule."

"It seems to me," said Kemal, "that he ruled rather well. He hamstrung my uncle for years by bequeathing the Dancers' voice to me."

"I am only repeating what Gordon said," Ramora said smugly.

"Uncle Gordon weathered my father's death admirably," said Kemal, unable to keep the irritation out of his voice.

"He said you would never know how he died."

Kemal turned on her, grasping her wrist in a painful squeeze.

"Ouch!" squealed Ramora. "Let me go! I'll tell Gordon!"

"No doubt you will," he replied tightly, "but remember one thing. You are a concubine. I am family, even if I am a black sheep. You can be replaced."

"He laughed when he said you would give half of Mercury Prime to know who killed Ossip, and that you had missed the answers to your questions in a prison cell." Ramora sneered again.

"You vicious little trollop!" Kemal twisted her wrist, and Ramora squealed. "What did he mean? Tell me!"

Ramora panted, her eyes blazing. "Never!"

Kemal wrenched her arm sideways.

She howled. "All right! All right. I'll tell you what I know."

Kemal eased his grip, but he did not let her go.

"A man named Egon. He knows about your father's death."

"Egon! The master Musician? I met him . . . in a jail cell!" The light of understanding dawned in Kemal's eyes.

"There! I've told you." Ramora tugged at her imprisoned wrist.

Kemal looked down at her, his eyes grim. "You are lucky, Ramora, you are dealing with an even-tempered Gavilan. Dalton would have torn your face off."

She smirked up at him, simpering, confident of her seductive powers. Kemal found her overtures nauseating in spite of her beauty, but he did not let his feelings show. She was a useful source of information. He cultivated her with a smirk of his own and grasped her chin in one hand.

"You are a tease, Ramora. You had best watch your step. It could get you into serious trouble."

"Or into your bed?" she asked innocently.

"As I said," returned Kemal. He let her go. "Now, run along. I have work to do."

She pouted at him. "It can wait," she said.

"One thing you should have learned by now, Ramora. A Gavilan takes pleasure, but work is his first concern. Now, leave me! I have no more time for you."

"Next time I won't be so easy to find," she said.

"Why, Ramora, of course you will. Gordon will see to that. By the way, did you find out what he wanted to know?"

Her eyes grew large with surprise. She whirled to her feet and flounced toward the door, her ample figure stiff with indignation.

"Be sure to tell Gordon how much I enjoyed our chat," Kemal said to her retreating back.

Ramora did not reply. The door closed behind her, leaving Kemal with his thoughts. She had given him valuable information, but he had little time to digest it. He began to pace again, running over the facts she had divulged. In spite of his imminent interview with Ardala, Kemal found his thoughts returning to Egon, the master Musician, and the unexplained circumstances of his father's death.

He went to his sleeping chamber. This was the room he remembered from his childhood, still filled with a child's toys and books. It was comforting, the only place on the whirling body of Mercury Prime where he felt secure. He sat down at the old computer terminal and accessed the Mercury Prime security computer.

"Prisoner roster," he said.

"Classified," returned the computer.

"Gavilan," answered Kemal.

"Identify," demanded the computer.

"Kemal, ben Ossip."

"You are not cleared for that information," said the impersonal computer voice.

Annoyance slashed through Kemal's eyes. His uncle was fond of touting his position as a member of the family, but it was evident he was a long way from trusting his nephew.

He reached for the keyboard and typed his name in lowercase letters. There was a shimmer beside him, and the ancient, slightly blurry holographic eye on his terminal created Ossip's tall figure beside him.

"My son."

"I need to override the security code for the prisoner roster," Kemal said.

"Try 'golden sovereign'," replied the hologram.

Kemal dutifully entered the code.

"Accepted," answered the computer.

Kemal's inquiry complete, the holographic eye deactivated, and Ossip was gone.

A list of names ran quickly across the screen. Kemal checked them eagerly, but Egon's name was not among them.

"Records," he said. "Access a file on a prisoner named Egon."

The computer hummed, then replied, "That file is inactive."

"Released or dead?" he asked, trying to curb his annoyance with the literal machine.

"Released," answered the computer.

So Egon still lived—at least as of his release date. Gordon was fond of banishing his political prisoners to the surface, expecting them to die quickly. Kemal had a feeling Egon would not succumb easily to the elements. He scrolled Egon's file across his computer screen, noting the years of his incarceration. They ran from the year of his father's death to his own stay in Mercury Prime's detention center. "Released at Giotto's Edge, near the entrance to Giotto Warren," he read. He filed the information, intending to follow up on it once his negotiations with Ardala were completed.

The lovely vampire intruded upon his thoughts, and he concentrated on a plan to outwit her.

O   O   O   O   O

Dalton Gavilan was checking over the systems of his personal fighter, methodically going through the list. He had no intention of being left behind because of a malfunction. He intended to stay on Kemal's tail all the way to Tortuga, flying beyond sensor range so his esteemed cousin would not know he was there.

"Oh! Sir! I thought 'twas a thief!" The watch, a member of Gordon's personal guard, raised his portable light so it shone on Dalton's face.

Dalton squinted into it. "Do you have to blind me with that thing?" he asked irritably.

"Sorry, sir." The man dropped the lantern. "Anything I can help you with, sir?"

"You can release the nuclear fuel lock. I want to make sure she's topped off before I sleep."

"But, sir, regulations—"

"Do you disobey me?" Dalton rose to his full height, his powerful shoulders squaring aggressively.

"No, sir!" answered the guard. "Only take me a moment, just have to find the right key." He fumbled with the keys on a cord around his neck, selected one, and went to a steel cage built around three huge tanks. He unlocked the cage and went in. "Fuel on number one tank," he said.

Dalton punched the number one on the fuel outlet beside his ship, lifted the nozzle out of its holder, and shoved it into the open tank. The fuel, converted into energy in a nuclear fusion converter, gurgled heavily as it was pumped through the system. He listened to the tank fill idly, his mind on Kemal.

He had never trusted Kemal. Part of that, he knew, came from the fact that Kemal was the son of the previous king, and therefore equal to Dalton in stature. They were both firstborns. Dalton did not deal tolerantly with competition. His first instinct was to eliminate it. Circumstances prevented him from eliminating Kemal—at least for a time.

He relished this opportunity to shadow him, hoping for some bit of information that would convince his father that Kemal was a liability to the cause. Kemal's broken link to the Dancers made his position with the Gavilans less than secure. He needed the successful completion of this transaction with Ardala to cement his position with the family.

The fuel line clicked off, and Dalton lifted the nozzle from his tank. He flipped the lid down and locked it, then replaced the hose. "Done!" he called, and the guard nodded from his position next to the storage tank. Dalton watched him lock up the fuel supply. The guard returned to him, his manner respectful.

"Can I escort Your Honor to your quarters?" he asked, tactfully indicating that Dalton's presence on the docks was irregular.

Dalton smiled. "No. I have some tests to run before I sleep. You may return to your duties."

The guarded nodded reluctantly. Dalton's actions were expressly forbidden, but he was a Gavilan, and Gavilans were not to be questioned. He resumed his tour of the docks, noting his meeting with Dalton and a record of their conversation in his log. He had learned to be prepared, even when irregularities included royalty.

Dalton watched his reluctant departure, enjoying the man's uncertainty. He thought of the verbal drubbing the guard would receive from his superior and grinned. Rules were rules. They were meant to be obeyed.

Opposite Dalton's craft was Kemal's ship. The ship's streamlined hull and plain coloring offended Dalton. Kemal did not have the passion for ornamentation that was characteristically Gavilan, and he had purposely chosen this unadorned craft. "Take care, Kemal," he murmured. "I will be right behind you the whole way. One false flight, and you will die."

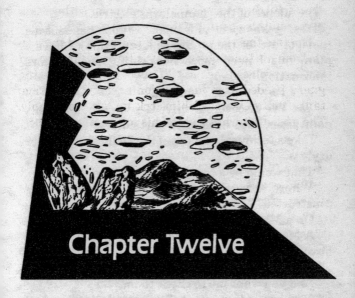

Chapter Twelve

Kemal cleared Mercury Prime and skirted the Mariposas. When the sensors showed him in clear space, he coded a secure frequency into his communications link, set it to scramble the transmission, and said, "Come in, Shortstop." He had no idea what the code name meant, but he had heard Buck use it when contacting Huer.

"Huer here," came the immediate reply. "Buck—"

"Sorry to disappoint you," replied Kemal. "This is Kemal. I need help."

Huer's eagerness was subdued. "Your uncle has discovered your purpose," guessed Huer.

"Not yet, but I am on my way to an interview with

Ardala Valmar."

The silence of the channel was electric.

"Yes," acknowledged Kemal. "Gordon has sent me to negotiate for the prototype laser. I think I have a plan, but I need more bargaining power, more information."

"And that's where I come in."

"Yes. I've discovered where Gordon is building his giant laser, but I need more particulars."

"Like a technical readout of the facility," said Huer dryly.

"That would be a help," admitted Kemal.

"Where is this doomsday device being constructed?"

"On a Mariposa," said Kemal.

"A Mariposa?" asked Huer. "How precise. Do you have any idea how many Mariposas there are?"

"Yes," said Kemal succinctly.

"And you want me to check them."

"Can you pinpoint the power blocks?" asked Kemal.

"Of course. They are common knowledge."

"Gordon certainly picked a secure place for his experiment," said Kemal sarcastically.

"Who would think to look there?" asked Huer. "The Mariposas are a perfect hiding place. They are always visible, so no one ever really looks at them." Huer sighed. "It will be time-consuming, but I should be able to pick up signs of unusual activity or uncharacteristic power surges."

"I'm counting on you," said Kemal. "Wish me luck."

"You will need it in an interview with Ardala. She

does not often get the short end of the stick, and, unlike me, you are not immune to her charms."

"I've already had a taste of her," returned Kemal. "I am not looking forward to meeting the lady in person."

Huer chuckled. "If it's any consolation to you, even Buck finds her somewhat overwhelming."

"At least I'm not the only one," said Kemal.

"Hardly. Kemal, you must discredit or destroy that laser and inhibit Gordon from building another."

"I know."

Huer signed off, neglecting to mention his interview with Duernie. It was a distraction Kemal could not afford. The fate of the system was riding on Kemal's young shoulders.

Behind Kemal, matching his movements like a shadow, flew Dalton Gavilan. His ship was identical to Kemal's in configuration, making it easier to lose Dalton's ship in Kemal's electronic wake. All of Dalton's sensors were trained on Kemal's ship, looking for any unusual activity. When Kemal activated his communications link outside Mercury's sphere of influence, he listened in.

He was met with static and garbled voices. He tried to backtrack the source of the static, but found security blocks. Immediately suspicious, he ran though the charts for signs of other ships in the area. He was looking specifically for pirates, knowing NEO had managed a truce with the Rogues' Guild and figuring they would be safer for a covert operation than NEO's own ships. There was nothing.

Yet he knew Kemal was using a cloaked communications link. He had no need for a secure communications line, unless, of course, Ardala had contacted him. That possibility irritated Dalton. He did not want a reasonable explanation for Kemal's actions. He wanted treason. He followed Kemal, matching his movements expertly.

O O O O O

"I want passage."

Duernie's low voice was firm. The cloaked and hooded figure before her did not reply. In the dim light of a black corridor in the complex tunnel system of Tir Plantia Warren, the figure was a deep black shadow in the dimness.

"I was told to contact Rockbite," said Duernie.

"You found him." The voice issuing from the figure was a creaky falsetto, put on to conceal the owner's true voice.

"I want private passage to Mercury Prime," Duernie said. She hunched her slim shoulders under the cloak she wore, uncomfortable with the oppressive weight of rock above her. The warren was dug deep beneath Mercury's surface.

"When," asked Rockbite.

"Soon," replied Duernie. "My business is urgent."

Rockbite extended a gloved hand. "Pay now."

Her characteristic frown deepening, Duernie placed a stack of gold and silver Venusian coins in Rockbite's hand. She had come prepared, knowing her dealings would be in person. Her logical nature rebelled at payment in advance, but she knew it was the only way.

Rockbite's fist closed around the money. "I will

send word. Coordinates?" he asked.

"They are with the payment," replied Duernie.

Rockbite nodded, then froze, head cocked. "Warren guards!" he hissed. "You brought them to trap me!"

"No!" said Duernie. "I must get out of here!" She whirled to a side corridor and ran down it.

For a split second, Rockbite watched her go, shaking his head, then melted into the shadows of the main tunnel.

Duernie ran, her feet making far too much noise in the tunnel. She could hear pursuing feet, but her sense of direction was confused by the caverns. She dodged into another tunnel and almost ran over two guards.

One man went sprawling as she hit him, his hand light crashing into the rock wall. It went out, and the corridor darkened. These back passages were seldom-used access tunnels for the warren's maintenance systems, and they were lit by small solar dots. Shadows danced wildly in the half light.

Duernie struck the second guard as he reached for his sidearm, breaking his arm with a single well-placed blow. He howled and grabbed for her, but she clasped her hands and landed a solid punch to his stomach. He doubled up, helpless with the wind knocked out of him.

She darted by him, but the first guard caught her by the ankle. She went down reaching for her dagger, the gold hilt smooth in her hand. As the guard strove to pin her arms, she slid the blade under his jawbone.

"Let me go!" she said tightly. The man's grip eased. She slid away from him, her knife still at his throat. "Wrist irons," she said.

The man fumbled for the handcuffs at his waist, then held them out to her.

She shook her head. "Clip one on," she ordered. "Then on your stomach!"

He complied, and Duernie knelt in the middle of his back, fastening his hands behind him. The whole operation had taken seconds. Duernie did not stop to admire her handiwork. With all a Dancer's grace, she ran down the corridor.

Chapter Thirteen

Kemal negotiated the approach to Tortuga carefully. The Tortuga controller had given him precise landing coordinates, and he followed them to the letter, knowing that if he did not, he risked disintegration. Free ports ran on their reputations. That meant freedom for everyone who called there, no matter what side of the law he or she courted. That freedom was maintained by a voluntary discipline that made martial law seem lenient.

Kemal edged his Mercurian cruiser up to the private slip. A green light came on at the front of the slip as docking magnets activated. The ship was pulled smoothly in, anchoring with gentle clicks. The green

light changed to red, and a worker darted out to tie
the ship off, giving it double security. Kemal clipped
down his helmet, punched in life-support, and
dropped his restraints. The ship was at zero gravity,
and he swam toward the hatch, using the handholds
set into the hull. He reached the hatch and deactivated the lock.

Twirling the door mechanism, he pulled the hatch
open. The worker, clinging to the ship with his magnetized boots, handed him a safety line. His own
trailed behind him like a twisted umbilical cord.

"First entry left," said the worker, gesturing.

Kemal nodded his thanks and hauled on the line,
pulling himself onto the dock. He touched his suit
controls, and the magnets in his shoes activated,
sucking him down to the dock. He clumped slowly toward the doorway, knowing Ardala could see his
every movement. The enforced ponderousness of his
approach put him on the defensive.

He reached the doorway and knocked. The red light
above the door blinked in reply, then went green. He
grasped the door handle and wrenched it sideways,
then pulled the door open and stepped into the ante-
chamber. He closed the door behind him, locked it,
and a green light overhead began to blink. When it
stopped, he heard a warm, feminine voice.

"Welcome to Governor's Garden. Life-support is op-
erative. You may remove your helmet."

Kemal followed instructions, unclipping his helmet and shoving it under his arm in the time-
honored manner of all supersonic pilots. The door
into the villa slid open from the center, and Kemal
stepped into a world of tropical splendor, all white

walls and latticework, lush plant life, and exotic birds. A huge purple moth flew heavily by, to cling to the lattice on the opposite wall like a decoration.

"Governor's Garden," murmured Kemal. "All it needs is a waterfall and a harem."

"Will I do?"

Kemal started at a voice like flowing honey. Ardala Valmar stood at a turn in the corridor. She wore wild tropical colors that rivaled the hues of the birds squawking in their aviaries. Her sarong fell off one shoulder to knot at the hip, showing firm white thigh. Laced sandals of red leather imprisoned her bare legs. Her full bosom threatened to escape confinement with every breath. She had brushed her hair to one side, catching it with a clutch of flowers over the ear. Her seductive mouth was painted rich red.

Kemal bowed shortly, knowing he was at a disadvantage. "Kemal Gavilan," he said formally.

Ardala advanced on him in an undulation that was hypnotizing. Even the soft click of her magnetized sandals was seductive. "Ardala Valmar."

"Um, yes," said Kemal.

She stopped before him, her tilted cat's eyes half closed, then reached for his flight suit. Before he realized her intention, she had popped the closures by pulling the suit apart at the neck. He caught her hand as she slid the suit back over his shoulders.

She smiled. "You don't look comfortable," she said. "I find it impossible to do business unless I am comfortable."

Kemal found his breathing was quick, and the fact angered him. He did not release her hand, and he forced challenge into his eyes.

Ardala released him slowly.

Kemal smiled ironically and finished what she had started, clipping the suit to a rack near the door. His fitted brown silk shirt and slacks were much more becoming, though plain next to Ardala's butterfly finery.

"That's more like it," said Ardala.

Kemal cocked an eyebrow, knowing he must maintain a semblance of control, no matter how fast his heart was beating. Ardala was more than a man should have been asked to face, even for the security of the solar system. "I have heard a great deal about you," he said. "None of it did you justice."

Ardala was pleased. She loved flattery, though she was not impressed by it. She started down the corridor, her body close enough for Kemal to feel occasional contact from her movement. "Did you have a good flight?" she asked, making the pleasantry suggestive.

"Fair," responded Kemal.

"I hope you did not forget anything."

"It is not my habit to forget," said Kemal. "If you are referring to payment, I have it with me, in cash."

Ardala nodded, her shiny hair glittering. "Let me see." Her voice was husky with desire.

Kemal extracted the certificate and handed it to Ardala. She smoothed it between her fingers. "It is a start," she said.

Kemal pulled back in mock anger. "That is the agreed upon price!"

"For a laser," agreed Ardala, her black eyes calculating. "I think I can offer you more." She ushered

him into a private room full of simulated sunlight
and cushioned divans, then closed the door. "For this,
we need privacy." She pushed on Kemal's broad
shoulders, and he obediently sat down on one of the
divans.

"What more can you offer than the laser?" he
asked, suspicious.

Ardala slid easily onto the divan, moving behind
him until her head was at his shoulder, her firm
breast at his back. "A world," she said. "A world for
you to rule."

Kemal let his head turn slowly. "What are you
saying?"

Ardala ran her hand sensuously across his back. In
spite of himself, he vibrated to her touch. "I am saying you could rule Mercury." Her voice was heavy,
slick honey. "You are a king's son. Has it never
crossed your mind that your uncle Gordon usurped
the throne?"

"It has crossed my mind," admitted Kemal.

"He would have killed you, too, had you not held
the reins of the Dancers."

"Are you saying he killed my father?" demanded
Kemal.

"That has always seemed the most logical explanation for his actions," answered Ardala. She slid a
ruby-painted fingernail up his neck, making the
hairs stand up.

"What has this to do with the laser?"

"I have been known to support political causes that
appeal to me. I am as rich as a Sun King, you know.
There is more profit on Mercury than the Mariposas.
I hear there is a new crystal farm that is producing

high quality goods."

"Perhaps."

"Crystals are becoming a desirable commodity."
Ardala let her rich lips hover beside his ear. She was
enjoying herself.

"And for crystals you would support my bid for
power?"

"For crystals and a sympathetic hand in the government. My skills would prove a valuable marketplace for Mercury's considerable raw materials. It
could be a profitable union." She ran a hand down his
arm.

Kemal caught it, frankly because he could stand no
more without dragging her into his arms. Ardala in-
terpreted the gesture as a negative answer.

"You would do well to think twice before refusing
me," she said.

"I have not refused. What you say has truth in it."

Ardala regarded him clinically. "You have a good
nose," she said. The statement seemed irrelevant,
but Kemal detected purpose.

"My nose has nothing to do with my ability to overthrow the established order. The Gavilan house is notorious for the quality of its intrigue. Even now,
Gordon probably plots my demise."

Ardala nodded her lovely head. "Your cousin
Dalton waits off Tortuga for your return. No doubt,
he is curious as to our conversation. I do have other
options, you know. Dalton would like to rule
Mercury."

"Then why not pursue him?" asked Kemal, dropping her wrist.

"He has no imagination. You are much more

interesting."

Kemal turned on her, grasping the impossibly small waist between his hands. He knew she was not a young woman, though physically she looked in her mid-twenties. He knew she was surgically altered to produce extreme seductive beauty. He knew she was totally without heart or conscience, yet it made no difference. The temptation she presented was intoxicating. He slowly pulled her close to his chest.

"I will not be toyed with, Ardala Valmar," he said, and kissed her warm mouth violently, knowing his actions would attract her.

She tried to savage him, but he broke away, the zero gravity taking him a little farther than expected. "My terms," he said.

Ardala smiled wickedly. She was an expert in letting a man think he had won. She leaned back toward him. "Of course," she breathed.

"Produce the laser," demanded Kemal.

"In good time. You will have to come up with more."

"What!"

"Tell your uncle Gordon I had another offer, and you had to outbid it. We will exchange money for the laser in another twenty-four hours, here on Tortuga. That will give me time to arrange things."

"Things?"

"I can hand you a revolution, darling."

"At what price?"

"For now, that new crystal farm would be nice. Give me the coordinates, and you are as good as Sun King of Mercury."

Kemal turned away from her, acutely aware of the way her body followed him. "You're asking me to risk my life."

"You risk your life by being on Mercury. You are an embarrassment to Gordon. He will dispose of you at the earliest opportunity. And do you have any illusions about the affection your dear cousin Dalton has for you?"

"No."

"Then I suggest your only chance is to take the offensive and put yourself in a position of power."

Kemal nodded slowly, as if he had been convinced. The sharp edge faded from Ardala's voice like magic. "Then it is a bargain?" she asked.

"It is a bargain." Kemal turned to her once more and grasped her face between his hands. "I perceive you will be a good friend to have."

"Better than you know, Kemal Gavilan." Visions of wealth flowing from the plains of Mercury and the wings of the Mariposas into her coffers made Ardala's eyes glisten with desire. "I look forward to a long and prosperous relationship."

Kemal pulled her mouth to his and drank of her poisonous lips. He knew she was a liar and a cheat, that she would play him false and make a mockery of his masculinity, but he still enjoyed the moment. Duty forced him to play his part well.

Ardala's arms went around him, slithering over his body in practiced sensuality. She melted into his arms, her full curves in slow, maddening motion.

When Kemal felt his will begin to dissolve, he broke away. "I wish there were time," he said heavily. "But if I am to accomplish my task, I must return to Uncle Gordon with your ultimatum."

Ardala's bosom heaved. "Go then," she said, the

honey of her voice undercut by her innate calculation. "You will return." There was certainty in her voice. No man who had once tasted Ardala's charms had ever resisted her.

Kemal touched her full lips. "Yes," he said.

He rose from the divan, but Ardala did not. She knew the picture she made, stretched out on the pillows like a cat. She depended upon the impression to draw Kemal back. She was going to enjoy running him through hoops.

Kemal looked down at her, his eyes unreadable. "You will have your crystals, Ardala, but you will have to come for them yourself. I may be ambitious, but I am not a fool. I can tell you where it is and give you the means to take it."

"That," said Ardala seductively, "is all I ask."

Chapter Fourteen

The twenty-four hours did not pass tamely. Kemal, moving off Tortuga to contact his uncle, caught a glimpse of Dalton's ship. Ardala had been right about his escort, though he expected as much from his loving family. He would have to be doubly careful with his transmissions. Dalton's handsome, intolerant face, distant with distrust, was a continual reminder of the fragility of Kemal's position. Leaving the scramble on his communications link, he sent out a signal on Gordon's personal line.

"This is Mercury Prime security," said a distant feminine voice. "One moment."

"This is Kemal Gavilan. I do not have a moment,"

said Kemal with carefully calculated Gavilan arrogance. "I wish to speak with Gordon."

Gordon's dark voice cut into the channel. "Do you have it?" he asked, ignoring preliminaries.

"No. Twenty-four hours."

There was tense silence from Gordon's end. "I should have dealt with the spider myself," he said.

"She seems to want to deal with me," said Kemal. "That's part of the bargain. Also, she considered the payment I brought a binder. She wants five million credits more on deposit with her bank. She will check the availability of the funds, and I will give her the transfer code when she has given me coordinates for the prototype."

"Lascivious little cheat," Gordon snarled. Something about his tone made Kemal think he spoke from intimate experience.

"No doubt, she sees a chance to milk the Mercurian coffers," Kemal offered.

"No doubt. All right. She can have her money. I want that lens back. I will place the credits on deposit. Give her 'ransom' as the transfer code.

"Appropriate," said Kemal. "Why the change of heart?" he ventured. "You told me the prototype was insignificant. Now you barter a king's ransom for it."

"I have reconsidered," said Gordon savagely. "The Sun Flowers are unique to Mercury. Their ability to channel power cannot be matched. If I control the entire market, I will also have an exclusive on the lasers, and I mean to control the market. I don't want to hear from you again until you have the prototype. And, Kemal, should you fail . . . you will not return to Mercury." Gordon uttered the threat with a hint of pleasure.

"Perhaps it is Dalton who will not return," said Kemal lightly, and broke the transmission.

He spent the better part of the day in a quiet cafe, thinking hard. He was between a dagger and a handgun, caught in a cross fire of events and relationships. Tension was a constriction in his throat that made swallowing difficult. He sipped at a golden beer until it was flat.

He was playing a game of intrigue worthy of his uncle, and without Gordon's years of experience. Kemal's education had been strictly military. It had taught him strategy with a vengeance, with all its devious trickery, but it had been active, physical. This was an internal game played with emotions, and it did not have the virtue of instant success or failure. If you failed to flank your adversary in aerial combat, you died. Immediately, no quarter. If you failed to convince your opponent in diplomacy of your veracity, you might not know for years. The uncertainty was crushing, and Kemal knew he did not have the temper to enjoy playing the game.

Behind the danger that crawled over his skin was the memory of Duernie. He might die here on Tortuga, or be murdered by his family, and Duernie would never know that in his heart he had kept faith. He gulped down the end of the beer and went again to meet Ardala.

Ardala greeted him dressed in a translucent, floor-length sheath of white, which covered everything but left nothing to the imagination. Her blood-red lips were a flag meant to goad his passion. He greeted her diffidently.

"I see there are five million credits on deposit at the Bank of Luna," she said by way of introduction.

"As you requested," said Kemal smoothly.

"Yes." She lowered her head until her eyes were nothing more than a line of curling black lashes. "And what have you decided?"

"I have decided that I am my father's son," said Kemal. The words were two-edged, but Ardala could not know that. To her, they meant that Kemal intended to claim his inheritance.

Ardala smiled, her lips curving as she recalled a delicious memory. "Ossip was a handsome man," she said, and sent the full battery of her dark eyes into Kemal's.

Neither the compliment nor its implications were lost on him. "So that is why you insisted on my handling negotiations," he said dryly. "You wished to compare father and son."

"And because of your years," she acknowledged. "I am well repaid."

"As I wish to be," said Kemal. "Where is the laser?"

"First the transfer code and the coordinates to the crystal farm."

"The transfer code is 'ransom'," said Kemal, happily throwing Gordon's money to the wolf. "I will give you the coordinates when I have the prototype."

Ardala chuckled. "The prototype is tied to a space buoy off Tortuga, approximately four points off the main tower and thirty thousand miles low. Look for a royal marker on it."

Kemal nodded. "I am to trust you?" he asked.

Ardala slid one hand up his shoulder and around

his neck. "You can always trust me, Kemal, for a price." She breathed the words into his ear.

"And now I suppose you want the coordinates?"

Ardala let her hair tickle his cheek. She knew the scent of it was effective. "Of course."

Kemal reached inside his shirt to extract a thin security envelope. He broke the seal. "You'll find the coordinates here. You'll have to be careful, though. There's a tight security network around the farm and a security satellite in orbit above it, camouflaged as a Mariposa. I've marked the linkages. Blow them and you can walk in and take what you want, you'll have to destroy the satellite before you can get near the farm."

Her fingers closed over his as she took the packet from him.

"You must have quite a market for crystals," he commented.

"Just now it is acute. Rumors of the beauty of these so-called 'Sun Flowers' has fashionable collectors slavering. This will net me a major sale." She opened the packet and studied the contents. "This location is within striking distance of Mercury Prime!"

"I never said it would be easy," said Kemal.

A flicker of annoyance touched Ardala's eyes, then she evicted it. Kemal had given her a problem, not a profit, but she would not let him see her irritation. She would have more control over him if he thought her interest in him was superior to her interest in money. "You realize," she said, "I cannot be of much help until I have successfully obtained these crystals."

"I have waited years. What is a few more days in

the rise to power?"

"You are wise for so young a man." Ardala eyed him with a flicker of respect. "Like your father."

Kemal bowed in acknowledgment of the compliment. "This should be just the beginning, then," he said. "I must return my uncle's property or lose my head. When I hear of a raid, I will contact you."

She closed the packet with a snap. "There is no time for wine," she agreed. "Perhaps another time." Her arm was still around his neck, and she pulled herself close to him, lingering over his mouth in a melting kiss.

Kemal returned it, praying for her to break away. When she did, he could not have spoken his own name. Fortunately, it was not necessary. He turned away from her like a soldier going to war, escaping the room. When he was safely in the twisted corridors of Tortuga, free from her villa, he stepped out of the rush of traffic and leaned against the station wall, breathing hard.

"Never," he said softly, "has a man been asked to risk more. That woman is a menace."

○ ○ ○ ○ ○

Ardala, left alone, let her anger erupt. She threw the packet against a far wall, but it floated infuriatingly in the zero gravity. "Sniggering little whelp!" she snarled. "Someday I will destroy you for tricking me. Crystals! Crystals in my sight but not in my hands, where I can make a sale! I will not be cheated, you Gavilan pig! I remember your father, yes, I do. He pleased me for a day. You could not hold out that long!"

Ardala continued her stream of invective, berating
Kemal, his family, Mercury, and the entire male gen-
der in general. He had handed her a chance to make
more money in one transaction than she often had
made in a year, for she had a solid market for those
crystals. Even the expense of stealing them would
not take an appreciable bite out of her profits. Her
market needed crystals now and was willing to pay
for the privilege.

Because the farm was so close to Mercury Prime,
Ardala's usual sources would not touch it. She em-
ployed an army of mercenaries for such emergencies,
but none of them would risk a confrontation with the
Gavilans. They were too powerful and too rich. To
work for them was one thing. To work against them
was suicide, no matter how big the prize. Mercenaries were businessmen. They did not mind risking
their lives, but they never threw them away.

Ardala stalked back and forth, racking her brain,
her snug dress snapping with the violence of her
movements. She knew a moment of temptation. The
thought of using her own men crossed her mind seductively. She vetoed it. She could not risk overt involvement with such a venture. Mercury was a rich
market, and she did not want to lose it. Should Kemal's attempt to overthrow his uncle fail, she would
lose the Gavilan riches. Better to keep her role
concealed.

She needed someone who would take a high-stakes
risk. Killer Kane's green eyes mocked her thoughts.
He had the audacity for the venture, given a good
enough price. His and her liaisons were entertaining, and she was confident in his ability. He was one

of the best pilots in the system, and his own ship had
stealth capabilities that would enable him to get in
and out under the watchful eye of Mercury Prime
and still escape detection. By the time ground crews
relayed a visual sighting, he would be gone.

But Kane was not a man to risk everything for a
handful of crystal dust. He had no enmity against the
Gavilans, though, as far as Ardala knew, he had no
love for them either. He would not risk a strike unless
she could offer him more than money. And, though
she did not like to admit it, Kane was one of the few
men her beauty would not buy. He enjoyed her, admitted her appeal, but he was capable of walking
away from her at any time, and she knew it. It made
their relationship equal.

No, to attract Kane she would have to come up with
something else. Kane's mistress was power. Ardala's
eyes flickered as she thought of a way to entice him.

"Raj, get me Kane. Make sure the transmission is
secure."

"Yes, lady," responded Raj. He had been standing,
as usual, immediately outside the door. He was privy
to his lady's moods even when he did not see them.

Ardala opened a wall panel and waited impatiently
for the blank computer screen to activate. It was five
minutes before all the security blocks were in place
and a clear line to Luna had been established. Kane's
answering code flashed across the screen, and she
knew he was monitoring his calls, accepting only
those he deemed high priority.

"Answer, you arrogant snake!" she hissed. "If you
pass me by, I will set a virus on your communications
system you will spend months catching!"

The answering code, impersonal, emotionless, stared her down. Ardala stalked back and forth before it, her anger rising into boiling rage. When the code flickered, she turned on it. "It's about time! I am not used to being kept waiting . . ." Her words trailed off as a secretary appeared on the screen.

"I am most sorry," said the flatly polite secretary. He looked like a turn-of-the-century British colonel. "Mister Kane cannot accept your call at the moment. He regrets the inconvenience . . ."

"He will accept my call or my enmity," snarled Ardala. "Get him!"

"If this is an emergency, I have an override code . . ."

Ardala threw herself at the screen. Her long fingers punched numbers into the panel below it. The secretary vanished, and her own communications technician appeared.

"Lady?" he inquired, his clean Nordic profile dramatic against the communications console.

"Jump that security block, and while you're at it, fry it."

The technician complied immediately. There was a squeal from Ardala's screen, and the image broke up, revealing Kane's study. He was seated at his desk, reading a book. Even in her anger, Ardala felt a thrill at his beauty. Kane was a recruiting poster with a scar, his dark hair and white skin a dramatic contrast to pale green eyes that bored through her like lasers. He put a finger on the book to mark his place and raised his eyes to meet hers.

"Yes, Ardala?" he asked. "What do you want now?"

"What I have always wanted," she replied coldly. "The system."

Kane's devastatingly charming smile flashed. "And you want me to get it for you? I thought we had this chat."

"I have something new to offer."

Kane looked his question.

Ardala threw down her cards. "A weapon that could make you master of the system, and me its mistress."

"My dear," said Kane lightly, "you already are." His words were deprecating, but there was interest behind them, and Ardala knew it.

Chapter Fifteen

Ardala turned away from the screen, flipping her glossy, shoulder-length hair with the hauteur worthy of a queen. The analogy brought a smile to Cornelius Kane's face. It was more than apropos. Ardala was not only a queen of commerce, she had family ties to the Martian royal house. She was one of the few women he knew who could claim their airs were hereditary. "Come, now, my dear," Kane drawled. "How can you take offense at the truth?"

Ardala was standing in profile, her voluptuous figure displayed dramatically. Slowly she turned her head, her eyelids lowered as she sneered down her nose at the seated mercenary. "You, Killer Kane, are no gentleman."

Kane's dazzling smile widened. "I never pretended to be," he answered. "Besides, gentlemen bore you. You like danger. You like power. That is why you cannot resist me. However, we digress. What is this superweapon?"

Ardala stared at him in silence. She knew he was annoyed, but she also knew he would die before he showed it. "A laser."

Kane's green eyes showed his bemusement. "Laser? They're as common as asteroids."

"Not this one."

Kane made a deprecating gesture. "Powerful lasers are hardly new."

Ardala's sensuous mouth was bored. "If you have no interest in the project, I will contact another."

"There *is* no other, Ardala, and you well know it. If you could use another, more tractable mercenary, you would do so. You need me, and I am tired of playing games. Tell me the truth, or cease disrupting my privacy." Kane went back to his book.

Ardala watched him scan the page, turn it, and begin another. The fencing matches they fought were part of the spice of their relationship, but sometimes the pretense grew thin. Ardala's temper was ruffled, and Kane's indifference was like a rasp. "All right," she said abruptly.

Kane closed the book. "That's more like it."

"I am talking about a laser capable of destroying principalities. I have seen a prototype, and I have the plans. The laser was capable of slicing a ship to rubble. A larger model might do the same to a city. The

Mercurians have discovered a unique crystal. One
Sun Flower can focus twice the energy of any laser
now in existence."

"Impossible. Even if what you say is true, it would
take a number of crystals. And the calibration of the
crystals is too delicate. Every time one burned out or
darkened, its replacement would have to be balanced
with those still in the laser. It can't be done."

"It can." Ardala's husky voice was ripe with determination. "My staff assures me of the project's feasibility, and I have seen the laser in action."

"Then you saw a fluke, a lucky accident."

"No." Ardala shook her head, and her hair swirled
in a black cloud. "Each setting will have its own controls, and each crystal is scanned prior to placement.
Initial placement is ninety-six percent accurate.
And—and this is where you come in, my love—there
is a new source of crystals, a source that is producing
remarkably uniform and clear specimens."

"Which, of course, would make the calibration of a
giant laser easier." Kane regarded her with a mis-
chievous light dancing in his eyes. "Where are they,
Ardala? The rings of Saturn? Luna? The legendary
Vulcan?"

Ardala's eyes narrowed with anger, her full mouth
drawn into a tense bow. "Mercury," she said.

Kane laughed. "Under the Gavilan eye. Now, let
me see . . ." He looked thoughtful. "If I remember correctly, a high percentage of Mercurian energy sales
are brokered by one . . . Ardala Valmar. Surely that
can't be you?"

"You know it is." Ardala's voice was a snarl. She
ran a hand down her side, fingers spread, palms hard

against the curve of her hip. She itched to get her hands on Kane, and she was not sure whether she wanted to strike or stroke him. "There is no point in subterfuge. It will merely take up time. The Gavilans are a rich market. If the laser should slip through my fingers, I do not wish to lose as rich an asset as Mercury."

"I suppose I am elected to collect the crystals."

"Yes. You are a mercenary, allied to no one. I have the coordinates of the crystal farm."

"I am not a pirate, Ardala. I am a businessman. What payment can you offer? A strike on Mercury will bring Dalton Gavilan after me, and, though I have no respect for his pampered upbringing, he is competent. I do not want to be on the opposite end of his laser sights unless the stakes are high."

"You have always wanted power, Killer Kane. Here is your chance. This laser can make you master of the solar system. Every civilization will quail before it."

"Somehow, I cannot believe you wish to share this with me," said Kane lightly. "Power is your lover as it is my mistress."

Ardala shrugged. "If I could, I would do this alone. I cannot. You are the only man I can call on who is capable of helping me. You are the only man with whom I have found even a moment of satisfaction." She advanced on the viewer, her walk fluid.

Kane raked her body with a glance, letting a flash of desire show. He had no illusions concerning Ardala's altruism. Once he had accomplished her task, she would let him go. He respected her ruthlessness, and his own intentions were far from spotless. "Where is this prototype?" he asked.

"I had to throw the Gavilans off the trail," she replied. I sold it back to them." An evil smile pulled the corners of her mouth up. "Of course, I removed the crystals first. They have many more, so it will make no real difference, but the loss will anger Gordon Gavilan. I have the plans, safely stored in my computer. Once we have crystals, we can build our own laser, larger than Mercury ever dreamed."

"You sold it back?" Kane could not believe his ears. "Have you no head for strategy? You handed an adversary a weapon that can destroy you. This time your eye for profit may backfire."

"Perhaps, but I think not." Ardala looked straight into Kane's eyes, her manner a plea and a challenge. "Get the crystals, Kane. They will buy all you ever asked."

"Give me the coordinates," replied Kane.

"I am sending them to your computer. My source says security is high, and gives you exact locations to disable it. Once you've cut the security system, there should be no resistance. K— my source says the plant is largely automated."

Kane watched numbers appear on his computer screen, noting the location grimly. "Within eyeshot of Mercury Prime. No wonder you wanted me."

"We are going to be rich, Kane, rich in power." Ardala's dark eyes burned with desire.

"Yes, my dear, I believe we are," returned Kane. He had no intention of becoming Ardala's errand boy, but nor did he mean to miss opportunity. He wanted the laser himself. Ardala had the plans for it, and the Gavilans possessed a prototype. With two possibilities, he felt the chances for success double. Carefully handled, Ardala might be tricked into letting him see the readouts. If he could scan them, he would walk away from the transaction with the lens and crystals. He counted as a bonus the black eye his coup would give the Gavilans. He had no love for aristocracy, which lorded it over others not because of merit but because of an accident of birth. Moreover, Kemal Gavilan had been part of the NEO uprising that had given Kane a bloody nose. He would enjoy returning the favor.

"Then I suggest," said Ardala softly, "we meet to discuss plans. I am at the villa on Tortuga. It is a short trip for you."

Kane eyed her beauty. She was providing him with the opportunity he needed. "Of course," he said lightly. "It has been too long since we . . . talked."

"Much too long," agreed Ardala in a husky whisper.

○ ○ ○ ○ ○

Kemal Gavilan left Tortuga with his cousin an electronic shadow. Dalton's ship was close enough for the sensors to detect, but he was using the traffic of the station to mask his movements. It took Kemal five minutes to locate him, lurking behind a freighter on the sunward side of the station. As Kemal moved away from Tortuga, Dalton left the freighter and hugged the tail of a disreputable pirate ship. He was taking a chance, riding the tail of a pirate. The Rogues' Guild respected Tortuga's status as a free port, but Dalton's ornate Mercurian ship looked more like a rich prize than one of their own. Given time to think, they were likely to turn on it.

Kemal knew Dalton would give them no time to think. The moment Kemal was outside sensor range, he would set out after his cousin. Kemal sent his ship into space at three-quarter throttle, burning up the darkness. He hoped Dalton would think he was hot-sticking, indulging a schoolboy passion for a celebration of speed.

Kemal's speed was intended to put him beyond Dalton's communications link. He did not want Dalton to know he was making any transmission, much less decode it. He headed for a communications buoy, a satellite booster that amplified communications signals for transmission. He flew past it, then put the buoy in a direct line between himself and Dalton. If Dalton tried to tap his communications systems, he would have to sort through half the system before he found Kemal.

"Home run!" said Kemal, punching coordinates into the computer. The open communications line crackled, and he repeated the recognition code. "Home run."

"Ummm?" answered Huer's voice, vague with preoccupation.

"Huer?" asked Kemal, uncertain.

"Oh. Yes," answered Huer. "Bases loaded," he replied as an afterthought.

Kemal accepted the countersign gratefully. "I think I convinced her," he said. "We don't have much time. Dalton is trailing me."

"Are you sure Ardala accepted your veracity?" asked Huer.

"She gave me the coordinates for the prototype,"

Kemal said.

"I am opening a coded line. Send them," demanded Huer. "And let us hope the prototype is actually there. What did you have to give her for it?"

"Oh, I have to depose my uncle and take over Mercury. Then, if I am very lucky, I may be able to share a throne with Ardala."

"Got them!" said Huer. "Imagine her treachery. And you, Ossip's son."

"What does that mean?" asked Kemal.

"Ardala and your father had a stormy relationship when he was a young man—not much older than you."

"How old is she, anyway?" asked Kemal. "She looks so young."

"She is as old as evil itself," replied Huer. "Her genetic experiments have preserved her beauty, even enhanced it. But they have not improved her heart."

" 'More terrible than an army with banners,' " quoted Kemal.

"What?"

"Just something Buck once said about women," answered Kemal.

"Statistics tell me he was innately correct." Huer checked the coordinates Kemal had provided. "This position is accessible. I am going to have Barney pick that thing up."

Kemal was thoughtful. His recent partnership with the pirate had taught him the limits to which he could trust the pirate. "I don't suppose he'd sell it to the highest bidder."

"Not if I tell him the captain wants it," said Huer. Buck was an effective leash on the pirate.

"Here comes Dalton!" said Kemal. "I'm breaking off!"

Kemal cut the line, hoping he had disconnected the disguised channel before Dalton could detect his transmission. He sent his ship toward Mercury, his thoughts whirling with possibilities. If he could stall Gordon until the prototype was safely in NEO's hands, and carry out the ruse he meant to run, there was a slim chance to avert destruction.

"Come to give me an escort, Dalton?" he said flippantly.

His cousin's somber voice answered him out of the communications link. "I am here to ensure the safety of royalty," he said. "It would not do for an envoy to die. Negotiations get muddled in a murder. Was your . . . conference . . . successful?"

Kemal ignored Dalton's insinuation. "Of course," he replied. "I held all the cards."

Dalton laughed, a nasty chuckle that irritated the communications equipment. "With Ardala, no one ever holds all the cards. The lady is a cheat."

"Of the first rank," agreed Kemal.

"Dealings with her require a knife at your back."

"And I know you will always be mine," said Kemal, thinking Dalton was more likely to stab him than protect him.

"The art of war," said Dalton coldly.

Chapter Sixteen

Black Barney's *Free Enterprise* hung motionless and invisible off the coordinates Ardala had sold Kemal. With its custom camouflage, it faded into the panorama of space. The big ship was a RAM heavy cruiser, overhauled to fit the pirate's needs. Most of the huge cylindrical body was cargo space, for cargo was Barney's primary interest. The goods themselves held little attraction for him, but the money they garnered, free of restricting taxes, was his religion.

Since the cleanup after the Martian Wars, pickings had been slim. Commerce within the system was guarded. RAM, whose extensive trading network was the bread and butter of piracy, had pulled in its horns. It was maintaining its established trade routes, but the reckless speculation was gone. It had been RAM's far-flung subsidiaries, which sprouted, budded, and died in a day, that made rich hauls for the pirates.

A RAM miner hitting a rich strike meant money. The pirates would wait until the miner contacted his home base for transport, then blitz the claim, cleaning him out. Of course, there usually wasn't a substantial enough claim to support more than one run, but the money was easy. Barney smiled at the memory, his horrific face splitting as he bared his teeth. The smile widened as he considered the project Huer had given him.

He was to retrieve an experimental laser for NEO. Technically, his work for NEO was without immediate profit, but it was always entertaining. To snatch the laser from both Ardala and the Gavilans with one move almost made him chuckle. They were both powerful forces in the system, but they could not stand against the wiles of Black Barney.

Barney lounged in his captain's chair, his monolithic body comfortable in the seat. He had stolen a contoured divan from a rich politician, ripped off the arms, and replaced them with the control units from the original chair. He turned his head, his colorless eyes expressionless marbles.

Eric the Red, Barney's communications chief, caught the signal. "Project team ready for launch."

Barney grunted. "Now," he growled. He was looking forward to renewing his acquaintance with the Mercurian laser.

○ ○ ○ ○ ○

"I tell you, there's something out there!"

"Oppenheimer, you're seeing things. You've been in space too long."

"No I haven't. I've got better eyes than technicians half my age, and you know it. The lady saw to that." Oppenheimer hovered over the sensors, scanning the readings for unusual activity. Karl Oppenheimer was a small man, ideal for work in space. He fit into all those nooks and crannies in satellite maintenance drones and small space stations. His degree in engineering, plus a fanatical desire to master all types of machinery, had made him the head of Ardala's testing crew. Although most of her business interests were the abstract transfer of information, she sometimes happened on more substantial mechanisms. In that event, Oppenheimer went to work, providing her with a report detailing the capabilities of the object and the price level she could expect.

He and his companion occupied cramped quarters on the space buoy named Zeta on Ardala's maps. Its exterior was innocent, but inside the buoy was a miniature research lab. Ardala had installed the facilities to provide a remote base for space testing of her merchandise. She utilized Zeta rarely, so there was no suspicion concerning its actual purpose. At the moment, it was the site of extensive tests on the Gavilan's laser, which was anchored to one of the buoy's struts, just as she had told Kemal.

"It doesn't make any difference how often you look," said Oppenheimer's companion reasonably. Dakina was one of Ardala's pets, a pleasure gennie

she had tired of and retrained as a technical
assistant.

"There's fluctuation. Are you blind? Look at the
way that meter is undulating."

Dakina watched a needle quiver. "So it will not
hold a perfect zero," he said. "The deviation is less
than a thirty-second of an inch. Nothing is there." He
reached out a brown hand to adjust the equipment.

Oppenheimer's small, hard hand closed on his companion's wrist. "Don't touch it! The instruments are
accurate." He stared into the viewscreen.

Dakina's hand trembled as he pulled away from his
supervisor.

The breath of fluctuation his instruments showed
rippled across the screen in a wave of distortion that
scattered the stars. Out of the blasted starscape came
the *Free Enterprise*, its camouflage gone as it moved
in for the kill. "Pirates!" shrieked Dakina, his delicate features contorted with fear. He was one of Ardala's domination series, and he was conditioned to
react to physical authority with fear.

Oppenheimer glared at the approaching ship. "After the laser," he said.

"But it is the lady's!" wailed Dakina.

"So it is," replied Oppenheimer. "Stop that bawl-
ing!" He studied the approaching vessel. "That is not
a Mercurian ship. We are authorized to release the laser only to Mercury." He kicked in the communications system. "This is Karl Oppenheimer on space
buoy Zeta."

"Acknowledged, Zeta." The breathless female
voice was computer-generated, one of Ardala's better
bargains. It handled much of her vast communica-

tions network.

"We have an intruder. The ship is streaked with red lightning bolts. I believe her to be hostile. We are under attack."

"Acknowledged, Zeta." The voice did not change inflection. "Will report code danger to central."

"Hurry up about it," snapped Oppenheimer. "Or we're going to lose the lens."

"Acknowledged," said the voice for the third time.

Oppenheimer found it irritating. He did not want to lose the lens, and he had no illusions about his ability to protect it. The space buoy carried no armament. That was part of its usefulness, part of the reason it made a successful outpost. He could change its position, but it had the speed of a slug. He hoped the transport that had dropped him at Zeta was still within striking distance, for it was Ardala's own, and heavily fortified. Ardala would not look kindly on his failure.

"They're coming." Dakina pointed a perfect shaking finger at the pirate ship. A maintenance shuttle powered from the forward cargo hatch. It dropped like a slow, swooping bird toward the buoy.

Inside the shuttle, Arak Konii sat at the controls. Behind him crouched a worker named Bomber. Workers were incredibly sturdy. He was bald, and the green lights from the shuttle's control panel reflected off his shining pate and caused the nictitating membranes to close over his pale yellow eyes. The effect was uncanny. He could still see, though his vision was blurred. He wore a one-piece silver spacesuit with a single air tank.

Konii's thin face was intent on his job. He could see

the laser in his forward view port. Anchored to one of
the buoy's struts, it hugged the buoy like a child hugging its mother. He could see four coupling lines, and
he knew there might be more. "Get that thing on
your head and go stand in the space lock," he ordered.

Bomber nodded dumbly. "Sweets?" he asked
brightly.

"When you come back," promised Konii.

Bomber cackled gleefully. Food was the one form of
payment he understood. He bobbed his bald head
happily and picked up the helmet.

"Go on!" said Konii, his eyes on the lens. "Remember to put two lines on it."

Bomber patted the cable coiled at his waist and
nodded cheerfully. He plunked the helmet over his
head, clamped it down, sealed it, and trotted toward
the space lock.

Konii cut the shuttle's power and started to turn,
trying to put his starboard side next to the lens.
"What the . . . ?" he muttered as the buoy, a stationary object on all the charts, began to move. He
checked his instruments, and the buoy's course was
confirmed. The computer plotted it on a thick blue
line away from the *Free Enterprise*.

"I am not going to chase that thing down," said Konii. "*Free Enterprise*, this is Konii. Be advised, the
space buoy is moving. I say, the space buoy is
moving."

"We see it." Eric the Red's voice cut the communications line into splinters of sound.

Konii heard him muttering in the background,
then a growled reply that came from Barney.

"We're going to send a shot across her bow," said

Eric. "Hold your position."

Konii adjusted his controls. The *Free Enterprise* leveled a blast of laser fire directly into the buoy's path. The pulse beam pumped bursts of deadly light into space like a stream of white fireballs.

Inside the buoy, Dakina cowered under the computer console. Oppenheimer kicked him roughly.

"Get out of there! You're in my way."

Dakina compressed his medium-sized body into a ball, his head hidden between his knees, his arms wrapped around his legs. Each flash of light made him wince.

"Useless," snarled Oppenheimer. He swung the buoy to starboard, but the laser bolts followed him easily.

"Give up!" whimpered Dakina. "Maybe they'll let us live!

Oppenheimer's hand came down on the controls reluctantly. He hated Dakina's cowardice, but he had no alternative. Zeta ground to a halt, barely one mile from its original position. Oppenheimer waited for the pirates, refusing to acknowledge his own fear in the face of Dakina's terror.

Once Zeta stopped its flight, neither Barney nor Konii had any interest in it. They were after the lens. Konii swung the drone around once more and chugged toward Zeta. He turned the drone's starboard side toward the lens, gave Bomber a thumbs-up signal, and waited.

Bomber jumped out of the lock, his safety line trailing behind him. The fragile white thread was his security. He drifted toward the buoy, years of practice telling him the specific moves that would make the most progress in zero gravity. In one hand he held a cargo hook.

As he neared Zeta, Bomber extended the hook, deftly catching the strut to which the prototype solar laser was secured. He hauled himself forward until he could lock a short safety line onto the strut. Suspended between the drone and the strut, he began to attach the heavy safety cable to the prototype.

From the drone, Konii watched the operation, his merciless face impervious to the worker's danger. Should either of the vessels move, the safety lines would go taut, eventually pulling his suit apart. It would not be an attractive death, but Konii did not give the possibility a second thought. He concentrated on Bomber's movements, ticking off each line secured and each line released.

Finally the laser was safely anchored to the shuttle. Bomber slipped the short safety line that had enabled him to work on the shuttle, pushed himself away from the buoy, and began to follow the shuttle cable back to his craft. It took long moments before he reached the space lock and descended.

The moment Konii heard the lock begin to pressurize, he cut in the engines, swinging the craft around in a slow arc toward the mother ship. He had to make his movements smooth, or, instead of towing the buoy, he would create a projectile capable of severe damage. To avoid battering the shuttle, he had to move what seemed like an inch at a time, all the while hoping the buoy was as defenseless as it looked.

The *Free Enterprise* moved to meet its shuttle, the forward cargo hatch opening to a mauve light. Konii followed Eric the Red's docking directions to the letter, knowing that one deviation could spell ruin. When the shuttle was tied down to the deck, the two lines on the prototype began to tighten, drawing it toward the ship's hatch. Ten yards out, a mechanized grappling arm reached for it, neatly clasping the prototype's base. The lens was pulled into the ship, and the hatch closed like a behemoth's mouth.

Oppenheimer and Dakina watched the procedure from the space buoy's main port.

"Will they let us live?" asked Dakina.

The *Free Enterprise* angled away from the buoy, its long body fading into a ripple of stars as its camouflage was activated.

"It looks as if they will," said Oppenheimer. "Of course, when Ardala finds we have lost her merchandise, we may wish we had had a clean death."

Dakina shivered.

Chapter Seventeen

Kemal sent his ship into the docking bays of
Mercury Prime with the confidence of a man
who knew that others must make way for him
in the name of a prominent birthright. Actually, his
heart was in his mouth.

Facing Ardala had been a challenge, but facing his
uncle Gordon with a total fabrication made him feel
like a small boy caught with stolen sweets. He knew
the feeling stemmed from his childhood, when Gordon had been a tall, foreboding figure in the background, a symbol of authority not to be breached.
Moreover, there was Dalton. Kemal had no idea of his
cousin's activities during the interviews with Ar-

dala. If Dalton had contacts on Tortuga, he might know more than was good for Kemal. Kemal knew Dalton's antipathy for him, knew that Dalton would grasp any hint of betrayal, making sure that it reached Gordon's ears.

"Docking complete. Ship secure," said a voice from Kemal's communications link.

"Acknowledged," he replied, and slipped off his safety harness. He took a deep breath and popped the hatch on the ornate Mercurian ship. The hatch door swung away from the ship and sank gracefully toward the ground, a handrail extruded from either side. Kemal paused in the hatchway, looking at his reception committee.

It was a picture of family solidarity. Gordon and Dalton stood shoulder to shoulder. Kemal reflected that Dalton must have pushed his engines to get back to Mercury Prime first. Behind the two men of power hovered Tix, slightly anxious, always insecure. Behind Tix stood Gordon's own guard.

"Hello, Uncle," said Kemal lightly, as he came down the gangplank. He did not acknowledge his cousins, and he saw Dalton's brow darken.

"Where is the laser?" asked Gordon, dropping all preliminaries.

"With Ardala. She wants more."

"Scheming witch! She is like a vulture, never satisfied unless she is picking the bones of a corpse. How much?"

That Gordon did not haggle, or deny her further payment, proved to Kemal as nothing else could that the Sun King had had previous dealings with Ardala. Kemal named a sum that made even Dalton's eyes widen.

"All right." Gordon's voice was tight. "I will pay it. But if I do not get the laser in prime condition, I will exact my own payment. When?"

Gordon's terse speech told Kemal how much the laser now meant to him. His uncle usually was a master of diplomatic turns of phrase. "Twenty-four hours. We will find the lens anchored to a space buoy. I have the coordinates in my shipboard computer. I thought it best not to broadcast them."

"I say we hit that buoy now." Dalton's quiet suggestion caught his father's attention.

"Ardala thought of that," said Kemal dryly. "She told me that if the lens is separated from the buoy before the appointed time, the whole thing is set to explode. We'll be picking up pieces of space dust."

Gordon paced the narrow confines of the dock, frustrated anger expressed in every footstep.

"What assurance did Ardala give of the condition of the laser?" asked Dalton.

Kemal cocked an eyebrow at his cousin. "Have you ever met the lady?" he asked. "None."

"Ardala bases her business dealings on a certain amount of good faith, difficult though it is for me to admit at the moment," said Gordon. "If she did not deliver merchandise as contracted, she would quickly lose credibility as a broker."

"This time, I want to lead the detachment," said Dalton. "The laser should be protected."

"Ardala specified all dealings must be with me," said Kemal.

"Go to Ardala! Make the payoff. I have no interest in anything but Gavilan property. You may become

Ardala's lapdog for all I care, but I will pick up the laser at the appointed time." Dalton's face was flushed with indignation.

Kemal repressed a smile. To have Dalton away from Mercury Prime during his ruse was a stroke of luck he had not anticipated.

"I am taking a detachment out in one hour. We will lie off the coordinates until the agreed pickup time."

Gordon stopped pacing. "Are you mad?" he demanded of Dalton. "Do you think the laser is guarded by a simple time bomb? Ardala does not work that way. If any hint of distrust reaches her, she is perfectly capable of blowing the lens, saying we were in breach of contract, and keeping the initial payment for her trouble. I intend to get something for my money. You will wait for twenty hours."

Dalton did not like his father's command, but he submitted.

"I am to meet Ardala's representative on Tortuga, exchange money for the code to deactivate the explosive device. I will pass that on to Dalton immediately." Dalton's averted eyes gave Kemal some pleasure. He did not like his cousin any more than Dalton liked him, and Kemal rarely had the opportunity to outgun him. To make Dalton dependent upon his charity was satisfying.

Gordon, his heavy face grim, reached out a square hand and placed it on Kemal's shoulder. His dark eyes judged his nephew. "You have done well, boy. I thought you too much Ossip's son, weak and full of pity. Bargaining with Ardala is no light task. Better men than you have come away worse. We will make the exchange. There are times when money is only worth what it can buy."

Gordon's accolade gave Kemal a pang. Yet he knew his uncle was trafficking in fire. The laser's sole purpose was destruction on a horrifying scale. No man had the right to hold that much power. "I have always been proud to be a Gavilan," he said. The irony was lost on Gordon, for only Kemal knew that he was referring not to his ruthless uncle but to the father who went beyond power's limits.

Gordon clapped him on the shoulder. "Come! You must get some rest. There can be no mistakes tomorrow."

"Soon," said Kemal. "I want to check the ship."

Gordon nodded, pleased at Kemal's military priorities, and left the dock, his guard trailing him like a puppy. Dalton hesitated, then followed his father.

"C-C-Can I stay, Kemal?" asked Tix, who had not dared to interrupt the conversation of his family.

Kemal looked surprised. "Of course, Tix."

"I don't suppose you've b-been able to talk to Father."

"I mentioned your interest in the lens. I am afraid he did not express himself favorably."

Tix slumped. "He never d-does. He thinks I'm incompetent. He's right. I have no aptitude for war."

"Then why try?" asked Kemal reasonably. "You are doomed to failure if you attempt only that for which you have no heart. You are an artist, Tix. Face it. Use it. I suspect your work will last beyond Gordon's—or mine."

A pleased smile made Tix's plain face attractive. His eyes sparkled. "Do you really think so, K-Kemal?"

"I do. However, do not expect laurels from your family. They will not understand. You will have to seek a larger audience, and your own friends."

Tix's face fell. "I have no f-friends. I have nothing in common with Father's and D-Dalton's military friends, and other people are afraid of me because I am a G-G-Gavilan."

"To be an individual takes more courage than anything else," said Kemal. "You will face ridicule and jealousy, but, if you are not afraid, you may have the reward of a few real friendships."

Tix hung his head. "I am afraid," he said. "I am afraid I will d-disappear, like so many others."

Kemal put a hand on Tix's arm. "We all disappear in the end, Tix. Those who are lucky can choose their course."

Tix nodded. "I think, K-Kemal, I will try." His smile was shaky. "I may not be very good at it, but I will t-try."

"That," said Kemal heavily, "is all any of us can do."

O O O O O

Duernie, in the privacy of a tiny room in Tir Plantia Warren's cheapest district, spread out the plans the computer had given her. They detailed a Mariposa and the computer block that fed collected solar energy into the transport system, which, in turn, relayed it to the general marketplace. Each power block had a system of electronic gates that directed the power. Not more than sixty-five percent could be open, or the transport lines would blow. Duernie had

found a way to open them all. The right supersonic
frequency would blow them, and, given a powerful
enough transmitter, the reaction could leap from satellite to satellite in a devastating chain reaction.
Mercury Prime's communications system was just
such a transmitter.

Duernie smoothed the plans, and the crunch of the
brittle paper was loud in the little room. Lit by a single dim panel, it was the cheapest and most unobtrusive accommodation she could find. It contained a
single pallet, covered with a thin mattress and a
blanket. It was a depressing hovel that suited her
thoughts.

Here the ache in her heart was dulled by ugliness.
The irritation of poverty distracted her attention
from memories of Kemal, and from the black hatred
she felt for him. But sometimes those memories intruded, bringing spots of sunshine into the room.
They were ludicrous, and she tried to banish them,
but they would not always go away.

There was a thunderous bang on her door, then another. Duernie jumped, startled. Her escapade with
the warren guards had put her on edge. She folded up
the chart she had been studying and shoved it into
the front of her suit.

"I'm coming!" she called. "Just a moment! I'm not
decent."

The pounding did not stop. "That don't make no difference to me," said a muffled voice from the opposite
side of the door. "Open up!"

Duernie put on her best terrified damsel face. It
was not as effective as it might have been, for her
strong features did not lend themselves to fear, and

her habitual frown was a deterrent. She knew she
had no alternative but to meet the challenge head-
on. She swung the door open.

"Open u—" The man's words were cut off as he realized they were not needed.

"What is it?" asked Duernie, her black eyes open
wide.

"I got a paper on you, from Prime." The man
smirked. "Worth five hundred. I come to take you in."

Anger flared through Duernie in a white heat. Her
rescue of Kemal had cost him nothing. He was free,
still accepted by his poisonous family, while she had a
price on her head. Probably one of the little ironies
that Gordon Gavilan cherished. She looked up at the
man framed in her doorway. He was six feet tall, and
broad, though a good portion of his weight was carried through the middle. He did not look bright, but
he was brute strong. She wilted.

"Come on," he said, misinterpreting her reaction.
He reached for her, turning sideways and leaning
into the room.

She was on him like lightning, delivering a blow
where it would do the most good. As he gasped and
doubled up in pain, she leaped by him and ran down
the dim corridor like a frightened hare.

Chapter Eighteen

Gordon Gavilan left the enigma that was his nephew Kemal, the soldier that was his son Dalton, and the disappointment that was his son Tix for the security of his private study. As the door closed behind him and the lock whirred into place, he felt the weight of leadership fall from his shoulders.

Normally he enjoyed the burden, liking the feeling of it as some men liked to perform manual labor. The administration of his empire was a satisfaction he had fought for and now cherished, but every man needed moments to himself. He went to a cabinet on the far side of the room. The doors were of precious black wood, and they reached to the ceiling. They had been carved with an intricate border of twining vines. The border framed a graceful bas relief of a young girl with a basket of flowers. Gordon regarded her sweet, distant features affectionately. Long ago, before he was more than a younger brother, she had been his wife and the mother of his children.

He opened the cabinet and took out a tall crystal goblet. It was shaped like a lily, but it was twisted, as the flower often was in the bud. It sparkled in the diffused light of the solar panels. He set the goblet on his desk and reached for a bottle of Martian claret. Distilled from impossibly perfect hybrid grapes, it was a gourmet's delight, rich and clean. He poured the wine, filling the goblet.

"Here is to you, my dear," he said, raising his glass to the carving. "You found in death a blessing, for you did not live to see the ambition of our eldest son, or the weakness of our youngest. I am only sorry you had to bear Roget's death. Had he lived, I might have a better successor."

He turned away from the carving, carrying the glass and bottle of wine to his desk, set them down, and dropped into his black leather chair. He swung his feet up on the desk, crossed them, and settled himself comfortably. He reached for his wine and swirled it inside the graceful cup. His thoughts were a tired jumble.

No one seemed to understand the importance of the Sun Flower laser. He knew Dalton viewed it as a military asset, but its strategic value lay solely in threat. Tix could see no use for it. As for Kemal, Gordon could not fault his actions, but he still did not trust

him. Deep in his heart he felt Kemal's loyalties to be
ambiguous, the reaction stemming from his nephew's decision to fight against Mercury in the Martian
conflict. Gordon shook his head.

The laser was Mercury's insurance policy in the in-
creasingly unstable political atmosphere of the solar
system. Once the device was operational, no power
would dare provoke Mercury to conflict. He looked
over the rim of his glass at the technical blueprint of
the giant laser pinned against the far wall. Certain
areas of the drawing were marked off, denoting sections of the laser that were complete. At this moment, even the satisfaction of that accomplishment
weighed little in the balance.

Gordon was tired. Being forced to deal with Ardala
Valmar was a blow he did not relish. He had accepted
her ultimatum with no visible sign of distress, but
she was a bloodsucker.

"Ossip, my brother," he murmured, "did you ever
wish to set the mantle down? Would that I had asked
you before you died." He sipped wine, savoring the
flavor of a summer day. His brother was long dead
and did not reply.

○ ○ ○ ○ ○

Kemal stretched. The luxury of a real feather bed
was heaven after the cramped quarters of space stations and spacecraft. He felt warm and peaceful, entirely happy with the world. Then he remembered
that he was on Mercury Prime, and that he had a
date with Ardala Valmar. The knowledge brought
him instantly awake, and the worry returned to his

face in tension around his eyes and mouth.

He was playing a lone hand. There was no camaraderie of the unit, no fellow soldiers to share the
burden or the blame. He could speak to no one, trust
no one. Even many of his friends in NEO must now
distrust him. He wondered about them all, but he
thought most of Buck Rogers. Rogers was not bound
by the rigid class structure of the twenty-fifth century, and he regarded a man strictly on his merits.

The last had weighed heavily with Kemal. Though
he had grown up away from Mercury and its pom-
pous display of wealth and power, he had never escaped the Gavilan name. Within five minutes,
everyone at the Ulyanov Academy had known he
was related to the Sun Kings of Mercury. In a day,
they knew his father had once ruled. Always, in dealings with other students or faculty, he had been
aware that their treatment of him hinged on his family's prominence in addition to his own actions. The
blows of discipline were softened, the commenda-
tions of achievement exaggerated. In the entire
school, there was not one person he could point to
who would be his friend under any circumstances.

Rogers had immediately accepted him as Kemal,
the man who knocked a hero flat at their first meeting. Royalty held no importance for him. He did not
care what Kemal's name or background could do for
him, because Buck Rogers did not depend upon the
charity of politics. He lived by his own actions and
was prepared to die by them.

Though his military upbringing had prepared Kemal for death, Buck's cheerful independence was a
revelation. It had changed his own outlook. It had

made possible his present predicament.

On impulse, he rolled off the bed and went to his computer. He regarded the keyboard a moment, then typed in the word "seal." The machine acknowledged his security block, then asked for instructions. He entered Duernie's name, requesting her file.

The computer thought slowly, whirred, and Duernie's visage, as severe and frowning as always, yet somehow satisfying, appeared on the screen. Here was the one other person in the system who was not impressed by Kemal's background. Her candor had been interesting from the start.

He read over the background material he already knew. She was one of four children, the black sheep of the family. Her father was a strip miner, poor in the standards of Mercury but able to provide for his children. Duernie had attended technical school in Strindberg Warren. Kemal ran down the list idly until he came to the last entry. It stopped him cold.

Staring back at him in gleaming white letters was the message "Status: fugitive. Credits for capture, 500, GG." Anger gurgled in Kemal's stomach, twisting it into a knot. He had not foreseen this, though he berated himself for not having anticipated it. His uncle Gordon had placed a modest reward on her head, probably for the aid she had given Kemal in his escape from the jail cells on Mercury Prime. He realized his luck in ordering Gordon's men to let her go when she had led them to the crystal farm. Royalty could sometimes outrank the penal system, but he cursed his inability to right the wrongs he had done her. He had not only handed her people over to his uncle, but he was responsible for her status. She would be tracked by every bounty hunter on Mercury.

Whatever sympathy his uncle's words had provoked in Kemal died a quick death. Duernie had stood by him in times of peril, had risked her life to save him. His family had tortured him, would have killed him if it suited their purpose. He knew they still would.

Kemal cleared the computer screen and typed his own name into the system.

"Kemal." His father's voice was deep, weary. His holographic image wavered in a momentary power drain as it stood beside his son's bed.

"Father," answered Kemal. He was not sure why he had accessed Ossip's digital personality, except that his father's presence, even secondhand in the form of a computer-generated approximation, made him feel less alone.

"What do you need of me?" asked Ossip.

Kemal sighed. "I'm not sure. Some answer. Some reason why fate deals a foul hand to people who do not deserve it."

"If I knew that, my son, I would know one of the great secrets of the universe."

Kemal was extremely tired. He sank onto his bed gratefully, some of his weariness absorbed by the down mattress. With his father's image watching over him, he knew he would sleep, and that was good. He would need his strength tomorrow. He also knew he would have bad dreams.

152   M. S. MURDOCK

"You lost it?"

"Yes, my lady." Karl Oppenheimer's voice was no longer sharp.

Ardala regarded her research team leader contemptuously, her glare hard.

"I am not a soldier, lady, and we had no armament. I tried to outrun the ship, but could not. I did not expect a raid. We have never been bothered before."

Ardala's eyes were full of black death. She did not like to be cheated, and she knew the Gavilans well enough to be sure of their feelings on the subject. They were paying a stupendous amount of money for the lens. They were capable of strafing her home on Mars in retaliation.

"You are right, Karl. I should have foreseen this. It was an oversight. As you say, our tests on equipment have never been bothered before. Could you identify the ship?"

"Our computer carries the readouts on known ships. It was a heavy cruiser marked with lighting bolts." He was breathing easier. This time, Ardala was not going to blame him for failure.

"A pirate," Ardala agreed. "And when they found the buoy could move—was a miniature space station—they still showed no interest in it?" she asked.

Oppenheimer shook his head. "They went right for the laser. Didn't even give the buoy a second look."

"Now that is interesting." Ardala paced back and forth in front of the computer screen in her office. Oppenheimer's anxious face followed her, but he said nothing. Behind him, Dakina stared worshipfully at his mistress.

Ardala turned back to the screen. "Did you sight other ships in the area prior to the attack?"

Oppenheimer shook his head. "No. Not for some time."

Ardala waved a hand in Oppenheimer's direction. "You are dismissed, Karl. I want reports on those two mining drones in three days. They'll be delivered to you in two hours."

"Yes, lady," said Oppenheimer.

Ardala let her eyes soften. She made her mouth into a moue of suggestion. "Get me the reports sooner, and there's a bonus in it for you."

"Yes, lady."

Ardala watched the light of resolve in the little man's eyes as his image faded from the screen, satisfied that her innuendo had done its work. She calculated that the reports would be in her hands in only two days. She sighed, knowing she could not dangle Oppenheimer at the end of her line forever. Paying him off would be a bore, but it was good for business.

Chapter Nineteen

Killer Kane checked his instruments. He went through the list methodically, leaving nothing to the hands of a mechanic or the wiles of chance. His *Rogue* was in perfect condition, its sleek scarlet body concealing unbelievable power. It was the repository of the latest technology, and its stealth capabilities made it virtually undetectable by physical means. The *Rogue* showed up on star sweeps as a blip of empty space so minute that only the most sophisticated sensors registered it at all.

Kane was a frugal man, yet he unhesitatingly spent millions on the *Rogue*'s care and feeding. It was his life, the link that preserved his safety in the void, allowing him to outmaneuver enemies and outdistance pursuers. Of all the possessions his vast wealth had given him, the *Rogue* was the one thing he cherished.

Of course, it would not do to let an adversary know his feelings for the ship. Such knowledge would make him vulnerable. Kane protected his affection under the guise of professional excellence. He was a master at his craft, a superb killing machine, whether with an unsheathed mono knife in a street fight, or in a battle of wits, killing lasers, wily smart shells, and rail guns. His life was always in the balance. He was therefore expected to be a fanatic in the maintenance of his equipment.

His clients accepted this. So did the men who worked with him. From the tiny ready room on Kane's estate on Luna, the two pilots he had hired to back up his strike on the Gavilans watched Kane's preparations.

"Look at 'im!" said Malone Quintzillion, a gennie from Spaceborne Enterprises. The company specialized in rocketjocks with superior vision and reflexes. "Think 'e'd get tired, wouldn't you?"

His companion shrugged. "Guess I'd rather have a wing leader who knew his ship than not." He was a Martian part-bred. His tall body was inappropriate to a fighter cockpit, but his mind was a lock-pick tactical storehouse. He worked for the job, not the cause. He had no loyalties.

"It's a point," conceded Malone. "Still, it's a bit nervy, him hoverin' over that ship."

"He's payin' you," said the half-breed, Poxon.

"You got that right." The gennie grinned, his

round face a genial moon floating above his black-clad body. "Payin' me enough to keep my opinions to myself?"

"I'd say that," said Poxon.

Malone bridled at Poxon's dry tone. "You got a problem dealin' with a gennie?" he asked. " 'Cause if you do, I can fix that right now." A slim stiletto appeared in his hand like a magic trick. The crystal blade glittered.

"I don't care what you are, long as you can fly and stick to my wing."

"Mmm." The gennie's quick temper was soothed, and the knife disappeared as quickly as it materialized.

Poxon gestured toward Kane, his long fingers typically Martian. "He told you what we're in this for?"

"Not yet," said Malone. "It's got to be big. The stakes were." He grinned again, remembering the pleasure his advance had bought.

"Your contract have a back door?"

"Only up to the start of the job. Yours?"

"The same. Once we take off, he can blast me out of the sky if I try to run out on him."

"The standard," said Malone.

Kane, flipping through the *Rogue*'s life-support systems, was uninterested in his crew's speculations. He had studied their files as he studied his ship, and both were competent, with solid references. Poxon was especially fearless, and Malone had a high success rating. Kane had already checked the two modified RAM fighters they were to use.

Like the *Rogue*, the ships were painted red. They bore no identification but a general space code number, which was a fabrication. They had been given stealth capabilities equal to the *Rogue*'s, and their boosted engines were able to keep up with Kane's ship. For this action, all the ships carried heavy laser armament, with mobile guns on either side of the up-swept tails, the wings, belly, and nose. They also carried smart shells, set with the coordinates Ardala had given him. In the event that Kane was disabled, or his shots missed their target, the smart shells would do the work.

He shut down life-support, satisfied of its efficiency. He relaxed in the cockpit, more at home there than anyplace else in the system. Ships were his first real love, and the only true one besides power. He thought of the lovely Ardala and her treacherous promises. Someday, he knew he would break her. In times of stress, he relieved his frustrations by imagining her as she begged for a place in his empire. It was a thought that gave him pleasure.

He knew she intended to come out of this transaction the winner. He intended that she should not. He wanted the laser, the plans, and the crystals, so he was speeding up the timetable. He would hit the crystal farm, take what was harvested, and despoil the rest, to make sure of his market. Then he would swing by the prototype's position. Though he had not been able to get the exact coordinates from Ardala, he knew the general area her research team frequented. He had swept the star maps of the area, pinpointing the satellites, buoys, and space stations within it. There were six.

He had instructed the computer to plot the most efficient trajectory between them, and had locked the course into his navigational system. He could blitz them long before the Gavilans were due to retrieve their property.

The clock in his head told him he had less than two hours until launch. He settled into his seat, knowing he could rest better on his ship than in the most luxurious bedroom his estate had to offer.

○ ○ ○ ○ ○

Kemal's military boots sounded a precise staccato click on the flight deck. He wore a one-piece spacesuit, his brown hair combed neatly, his hazel eyes serious. At the center of the launch bay sat his ship, again the ornate Mercurian fighter. As he approached the ship, he noticed a new piece of ornamentation. Neatly painted within the swirling patterns on the ship's nose was the Gavilan crest. He winced internally. The crest made him a sitting duck for every would-be kidnapper in the system, though he doubted Gordon would pay a fraction of a credit for his return.

At the end of the bay, his uncle Gordon waited for him, a forbidding figure in silver and black. He stood with his arms crossed in judgment, his feet spread. His stocky but well-balanced body was the same formidable outline Kemal remembered from his youth. He fought down an instinctive desire to duck his head in submission.

"Good morning, Uncle," he said pleasantly, keeping the words as light as his uncle's manner was dark.

"It is far from a good morning," returned Gordon.

"It will be a good morning when the prototype is safely anchored on Mercury Prime. I want that prototype returned. I want a working laser, no matter how small, in my possession. Its possibilities alone should act as a deterrent until we can finish the other."

"If Ardala keeps her word, you will have it soon," promised Kemal.

"See you do not fail."

The intonations of his uncle's voice were familiar. The memories from his childhood were disorienting, a *deja vu* that made time nonexistent. "I will do my best," he replied.

"You are a Gavilan," said Gordon. "You have made mistakes in the past, but you were young. Blood is thick, Kemal. You cannot escape it. You should not want to. There is not a man on Mercury who would not kill for your surname."

Kemal frankly doubted his uncle's final statement, but he did not doubt that Gordon believed it. He clicked his heels together and bowed from the waist in his best parade-ground manner. "It is a name I bear with full understanding," he replied, hoping Gordon would not question his vagueness.

"See you do. The fate of Mercury is on your shoulders."

Kemal nodded shortly. "I will do my best for my homeland," he replied.

Gordon nodded back, apparently satisfied. He moved back, allowing Kemal access to his craft.

Kemal walked past his uncle, feeling Gordon's eyes on him like surgical lasers. He did not react. He moved toward the ship confidently, the emotions churning in his stomach entirely concealed.

Gordon watched his nephew's course with impassive, dark eyes. He clasped his hands behind his back and watched as the ship moved toward the space lock and the lock doors closed behind it. As the sound of its launch permeated the chamber in a rumble of opening doors and fired engines, his son Dalton appeared at his elbow.

"I will give him five minutes," he said, "before I follow."

"This time," said Gordon, "take a detachment. There are two ships on standby. You never know what you might run into on Tortuga."

"There are pirates with NEO," said Dalton.

"Yes. There are also pirates who answer to Buck Rogers. And, despite appearances, I think Buck Rogers is still a very good friend to Kemal."

"I do not trust him," said Dalton blackly.

"Rogers?" asked Gordon, purposely blank.

Dalton hesitated before replying. "Kemal," he said finally.

"Oh. I do not trust him either. If I did, I would not authorize your mission."

"He has been asking questions."

"That seems to be one of his most irritating habits," agreed Gordon. "But remember, we cannot afford to lose him—at least, not now. He gave us the Dancers, but he still holds legal title to them. Until we can persuade him to sign over his right to represent them, we need him alive."

Dalton did not like his father's answer, but he admitted its accuracy. "I will make sure he delivers the laser," he said.

Gordon watched a second launch impassively,

heard the rumble three times as Dalton's detachment roared into space. When the vibration subsided, he turned away, his thoughts as twisted as the rings on his fingers.

Chapter Twenty

Prepare for coordinate transfer."

Killer Kane's voice was clear on his companions' communication links as he began final preparations for the strike on Mercury. The three ships were in the depths of space, headed toward their target. His wingmen still did not know their destination.

"Acknowledged," replied Malone Quintzillion and Poxon as one man.

"Coordinates transferred," said Kane as he punched the activate button.

"Course change accepted," reported Poxon.

"Malone?" asked Kane.

"My computer's questioning . . . there! Got it."

"Acknowledged," affirmed Kane. "Prepare to log it in."

"System clear," said Poxon.

"Clear," repeated Malone.

"On my word . . . one and now."

Like three swallows joined at the wing tips, the three ships swung around. They kept a precise distance from one another, pivoting on their tails. The performance was worthy of a precision flying team, but mercenaries mastered their craft for effect, not show.

"Course confirmed," said Kane once they had leveled off on the new trajectory, heading straight toward Mercury.

"We gonna fly by Mercury?" asked Malone.

"Cut the chatter," commanded Kane. "You know you won't be given a final course heading until we're well out. Right now, there are twenty possible targets within range."

The *Rogue* cut through space like a crimson laser, the two smaller ships hugging its wings, as obediently as chicks. Kane was running at full stealth. The option guzzled energy, but it meant they would escape most electronic detection.

"Sir," said Poxon, "my energy levels are dropping fast. I can't maintain speed and stealth without a stopover."

"None of us can," replied Kane. "I have two nuclear fuel dumps planned. Don't worry, Poxon, we're coming into this action with all the chips in our favor."

Poxon hated flying blind, but he was being hand-

somely paid to follow orders. Kane had made no
bones about the circumstances of this mission.
"Sometimes," muttered Poxon, "I let greed talk me
into things. Next time I will not listen."

As the ships cut through space, Kane calculated
their arrival time on Mercury. His blood began to
race at the thought of the danger, the excitement of
besting a fair adversary at his own game in his own
back yard. He controlled the feeling. It was not yet
time to give his emotions sway. That would come
later, when he cut through the Mercurian orbital
path, daring the messenger of the gods to outrun
him.

"My sensors are picking up something, off my starboard bow," said Malone. "Not identifiable yet."

"I see it," answered Kane. "It'll be within range in
two minutes."

"A ship?" asked Poxon.

"More like a detachment," said Kane.

"My computer just picked them out! Mercurian!"
said Malone.

"Course heading confirmation?"

"Course five-zero mark two away from us," replied
Poxon.

"Course `heading confirmed," said Kane. "Looks
like they can't see us." His voice was smug.

"What do you suppose they're doin' out here?"
asked Malone.

"Whatever it is, I don't mind, as long as it doesn't
ruin my business plans." He did not mention to the
men that his computer had identified one of the ships
as belonging to Dalton Gavilan, or the flicker of relief
he felt knowing that Dalton would not be on Mercury.

Kane respected Dalton's abilities and he had no wish to tangle with him unnecessarily. Fresh in his mind was the knowledge that Dalton had almost managed to best NEO in the final moments of the Martian Wars. Victory had been snatched from his grasp by Buck Rogers's nonchalance. A moment, a breath, and Dalton Gavilan would have been victor. Under other circumstances, Kane would welcome a contest with such an adversary, but not when it meant business.

Chapter Twenty-one

Kemal walked down Tortuga's twisted corridors, looking for a likely place to fake his
meeting with Ardala's nonexistent representative. The station was built around a central structure that looked like an old-fashioned wagon wheel,
but, over the years, the integrity of the original design was lost in a jumble of attached modules until
the station looked like an irregular cone. The path-
ways that had been constructed between the individual modules were narrow tracks that could
accommodate no more than two people side by side.
The tracks twisted up like a spiral shell, but they did
not have the shell's simplicity. They turned and

bucked, doubling back and forth before reaching the next level.

Kemal was on level two, where most of the more legitimate shops and coffee houses were located. He tried to move purposefully, as if he were going to an appointment, even though there was a knot in his stomach the size of a fist.

He knew Dalton had followed him again, though this time he had not been able to pick up his cousin's electronic shadow on his sensors. That worried him less than the knowledge that the Gavilans' spy network did not exclude Tortuga.

The station was populated by transients. Rumors swept through their ranks like wildfire. It had not surprised Kemal that Ardala had property in so disreputable a port as Tortuga, or that her elegant villa remained unmolested in a nest of cutthroats and thieves. She was one of them, he thought. Tortuga was fertile ground, which she cultivated assiduously. There were representatives of every major political system within its hallways.

Gordon's political spy system was not as extensive as Ardala's, but Kemal knew, from the moment his ship docked on the station, that eyes were upon him.

Ahead of him loomed a sign in elongated Martian characters. The handsome lettering made the Black Pennon one of those occasional sophisticated shops stuffed ludicrously between disreputable tourist dives. A free port catered to all tastes. A gourmet restaurant had the added advantage of cheap contraband goods. Kemal knew it would have the best imported Venusian caviar, a salty-sweet pickled fish that was one of his downfalls.

He ducked into the shop under an ominous black triangular banner. A smile quirked the corner of his mouth as he remembered it was one of the symbols of the Rogues' Guild.

The lone waiter scurried up to him, a white apron tied around his ample middle. "Table, sir?" he inquired.

Kemal gestured negligently to a table at the back of the room.

"I'm sorry, sir, but that table is reserved. Any of these—" He stopped in midsentence as Kemal slid a currency marker into his hand. "—but arrangements can always be made."

Kemal followed him to the rear of the shop, placed an order, and slipped into a chic mismatched chair. The Black Pennon's decor favored early spaceship. All the chairs were captain's chairs from scrapped ships. The name of the vessel and its final commander was etched into a metal plate on the arm of each chair, which still contained original, though inactive, control buttons. Kemal checked the big chronometer from a RAM battler hanging above the racks of crystal on one wall.

His food came, and he ate, feigning growing irritation. He ordered a glass of red wine and sipped it as the minutes ticked by. When he had wasted two hours beyond the time of the fabricated interview, he paid the bill and left, his frown and abrupt movements a sure sign of anger.

"Your food was not satisfactory?" asked the waiter as he made change.

Kemal leaped at the opportunity to consolidate his lie. "No! No, it was excellent. I am afraid my anger stems from a broken appointment."

"Ah," said the waiter, rolling his bovine eyes knowingly, "love."

"Worse," answered Kemal. "Business."

The waiter clicked his tongue in disapproval. "A woman who does not come—this breaks the heart. But an agreement broken—that cannot be tolerated."

"Unfortunately," answered Kemal, "this was both." He pocketed his change and left the shop, his nerves still on overdrive. He would not know until he reached Mercury whether his uncle would believe his tale of betrayal. He started down the corridors. The way was clogged with traffic. Kemal was not a big man. He managed to cut through the crowd, but his progress was still slow. By look and gesture, he gave every indication of a man wild with frustration.

A drunken pirate knocked him against the wall, and he grunted as a strut cut into his back. He ricocheted forward, when a small hand on his shoulder pulled him back with surprising force.

"Leave it," said a tough feminine voice in his ear. "You don't want to mess with that one. He's mean, and he carries a poisoned dagger." The hand slid around his neck in a caress that was close to a wrestling hold. "You got better things to do."

Only the woman's tone of voice kept Kemal from beginning the conditioned reaction his years of military training had drilled into him. She pulled him back, and her body was rock hard, without an ounce of superfluous fat. He moved with her, tense. "What did you have in mind?" he asked lightly.

She spun him around with a deft twist that told him she had practiced the technique. She grasped the short lapels of his black shirt.

Her look was a challenge. Kemal did not respond. Instead, he looked down at her tolerantly. She was short, the top of her head barely even with his collar bones. She was dressed entirely in black. She wore a contoured corselet of black body armor, and thigh-high boots. Her black hair was cut short and was trained to stand on end, so the top of her head looked like the crest of some exotic bird.

Her face was dead white and gaunt, with dark blue eyes burning hungrily in their frames of short black lashes. Next to the left corner of her small mouth was a tiny tattoo in the shape of a heart.

"I have no interest in challenge," he drawled, refusing to be ruffled.

"Then I can think of other things to do with you."

He caught the glitter of a dagger and felt its prick through the fabric of his shirt.

"If you mean ransom, I must warn you, my family would consider my abduction a simple answer to a complex problem."

"You're rich. And stupid. Only a fool or a Gavilan would wear real gold in this nest of thieves."

Kemal fingered the heavy gold chain at his neck. He was so used to the sight of precious metal that he no longer considered its attraction. He had made a mistake. "So," he said, "you go from kidnapping to simple robbery."

"I'm versatile," she answered, jabbing him with the knife until he backed into the doorway of an abandoned shop.

"You have such plans for me, I think I should know your name," Kemal said.

"You are just full of curiosity," she said.

Kemal slipped the chain from his neck. "And I am tired of being held at knifepoint." He dropped the heavy chain over her arm.

She snatched at the gold. "If you can give this up so easily, you are more than rich."

"Yes. But if you are wise, you will take it and go."

"When there is more? Do you think me a fool?" She laughed coldly.

Kemal's move was so fast that she could not detect it. One moment he was being held at knifepoint, the next he had his assailant in a painful hold. Her hand spread into a claw and the dagger clattered to the floor. She struggled momentarily, then realized he was not only strong, but better trained than she had supposed. She ceased to writhe, but her body remained tense.

"Or," Kemal finished, "you will find yourself with nothing." He shifted his hold and picked the chain out of her fist.

"Who are you?" demanded the young woman.

"And now civility." He shook his head in wonderment. "You are a creature of surprises. I want answers, now! Your name!"

She regarded him sullenly. "Blackthorn," she said. "My friends call me Blackie."

Kemal nodded, not surprised at the lack of a surname. "Why did you pick me?" he asked.

"You looked easy. I was wrong."

"No one pointed me out?"

She shook her head.

He pushed her away from him. She stumbled across the room and crashed into the opposite wall. She caught her balance and her eyes sought the door.

"Blackie."

Kemal's voice stopped her.

He tossed her the chain. "For luck."

She caught the chain, her eyes full on Kemal's face. Instead of trying to escape, she advanced on him. Once again she grasped him by the lapels, but this time she did not speak. Her eyes were unreadable. "I can be a profitable person to know," she said.

"And dangerous."

"Will you tell me your name?"

"Kemal Gavilan."

Her thin eyebrows shot up. She chuckled, and the sound was not unpleasant. "I was more correct than I knew."

Kemal nodded. "You are speaking with a fool." He caught her shoulder. "Tell me one thing. Have you heard any rumors about me?"

She sucked in her already gaunt cheeks in concentration. "Something about your loyalty to NEO. I can't remember what. Now that I know who you are, I can keep my ears open."

On a whim, Kemal threw out a question. "Have you ever heard of Ossip Gavilan?" he asked.

"Sure," responded Blackie. "The old king. Tortuga isn't off the beaten spaceways. I know a man who used to work for him."

Kemal grabbed both her shoulders. "Tell me his name."

"Egon," she replied, mystified.

"Do you know where he is?"

"Sure." Blackie narrowed her brilliant blue eyes in suspicion. "What do you want with him?"

"Talk," said Kemal shortly.

"He left Mercury because his life was in danger. How do I know you don't want him dead?"

"You don't. But I don't." Kemal's slow smile lit up his face. "I have been looking for him for some time. Blackie, we met in prison on Mercury. I mean him no harm."

She studied his face. "All right," she said. "But if any harm comes to him because of you, I will hunt you through the system. He befriended me when no one else would."

"Your words are an echo of my own," he said. "Let me speak to him."

Blackie shoved the chain into a tight pocket and motioned for him to follow her.

As Kemal started after her, memories of his father haunted him. Ossip had died while Kemal was still a child, and the fact had been combined with fiction to produce the picture Kemal carried in his head. When he tried to sort what he had been told from actual fact, he was left with fragments: a strong hand helping him up when he tumbled down the stairs; the smell of perfumed cloth and the slick feel of precious metal; a voice sometimes sharp but always firm, guiding him through a formal reception; strong arms that made him feel as if nothing in the world could hurt him.

The memories were distant, but they brought a mist to his eyes. Ossip had not lived long enough for his son to know him as a man. Yet Kemal knew the tie of blood, and he could not rest until Ossip's murderer was brought to justice. In spite of the gravity of Kemal's present position, his father's spirit called for rest, and Kemal heeded the summons.

Chapter Twenty-two

Kemal found himself in a cramped two-room apartment that reminded him of the illustrations in his childhood storybooks, all colors and carpet. The walls were covered with fabric, the rich textures hung by bolt width, so the walls were a pattern of stripes in blue and green and warm beige. Some of the cloth was edged with bands of gold, which made dramatic accents. The floor was covered with thick beige carpet, and hand-woven rugs, like blue and green and pink jewels, were scattered over it. There were no chairs, only piles of pillows stacked against the walls, like a bedouin's tent. A metal lantern, its intricate scrollwork design breaking up the light from the solar panel it contained, made a dappled pattern on the walls. Seated on a pile of rugs, an ancient stringed instrument in his hands, was a man Kemal remembered. The man's eyes were closed, and he was humming softly.

Kemal opened his mouth to speak, but Blackie shook her head, putting a finger to her lips in a symbol for silence. Kemal held his tongue, hoping the old man was not senile and they would not be standing in respectful silence for hours.

Egon, master Musician, strummed the instrument lightly, his silver hair gleaming under the light. He wore a loose Musician's tunic in dark red. It was belted at the waist with black web, held with a plain brass buckle. He had settled on Tortuga, the nearest free port to Mercury, because on a free port no one asked questions. He hummed the final bars of his composition and opened his eyes.

"Kemal Gavilan," Egon said. There was no suspicion in his voice.

"You know him!" Blackie blurted. "He said so, but you can't trust what a man says."

"I am inclined to trust this one," replied Egon, "despite the rumors I hear of his defection from NEO."

Kemal, who had wanted nothing more than to talk to Egon, was silent under the accusation. He could say nothing in his own defense without jeopardizing his attempt to destroy the solar laser.

"I thought you wanted to talk to him," said Blackie. There was amusement in her blue eyes.

"I do," Kemal professed.

"Your wants may not coincide with mine," said Egon. "Why should I speak with a man who, I have been told, would turn his back on his friends?"

"You said you were inclined to trust me."

"Yes. I did not say I would."

Kemal looked down at the old man. "I cannot explain my actions," he said. "I can only hope they are for the best."

Egon looked at Kemal, his clear eyes on the younger man's face. "Sit," he said at last.

Kemal sank gratefully to the floor, Blackie close beside him. "This is considerably more pleasant than our last meeting," he said.

Egon chuckled. "Considerably."

"I came to ask you about my father."

Weariness settled over Egon's features. "I was afraid of that. I have been expecting it for a long time. Frankly, it surprised me you did not question me while we languished in that prison cell."

"I was younger," said Kemal. "More ignorant."

"Ah," said Egon. "The beginning of wisdom: the knowledge that we can never know."

"But I want to know about my father," said Kemal.

"About his death," amended Egon.

"Yes."

"Ask your questions," said the Musician slowly.

"Was he murdered?" asked Kemal bluntly.

Egon's mouth tightened into a straight line. "I think so," he answered.

"But you do not know?"

"If you mean was I an eyewitness to the deed, no, I was not. I saw Ossip an hour before his death, and he was as hale as you. I am not saying he would not have died of natural causes, but I doubt it. Circumstances were too advantageous for Gordon's rise to power, and the others refused to show the body."

"You think Gordon murdered him," Kemal said shrewdly.

"I think Gordon was the reason for his murder. Whether he actually killed Ossip himself, that I cannot say. He is capable of it, particularly if he convinced himself he was doing it to safeguard Mercury. He and Ossip had major political differences, prominent among them the Dancers' place in the scheme of things."

"So Ossip signed the Dancers over to me to protect them."

"Yes. Under the terms of the agreement, they were in your hands and could not be administered by a regent."

"My father trusted a child's judgment more than his own brother's. That's interesting."

"But he did not tell you of your power."

"That," said Kemal wryly, "is no doubt the reason my dear uncle Gordon sent me away to school. Had I remained on Mercury, I would have discovered it."

"And become a perfectly obnoxious, spoiled brat," interjected Blackie.

"Like you?" asked Kemal mildly.

"Stroke," said Egon. "I don't think you can push this one around, Blackie."

She subsided, but her glare was not convincing.

"Kemal, I wish I could be more help to you," continued Egon. "I have little more than the common rumors of the day. I saw nothing."

"Then why," asked Kemal, "are you afraid for your life? Why were you in prison?"

"I have always assumed I was part of the general

purge. It's not discussed much now, but quite a few of your father's supporters lost their lives soon after he did."

Kemal leaned back against a gold pillow. It showed off his black shirt and slacks to good effect, picking up the color of the gold embroidery on the shoulders of the shirt. He narrowed his eyes. "A purge is short lived. A man who makes it through the first year will usually be out of danger, but you seem convinced you are still hunted. You must know something."

"But what? Don't you think I've tried to figure it out?" asked Egon, frustration in his rich baritone voice.

"Will you go over the details of your last meeting with my father? Aside from discovering something, I would really like to know his final hours."

"Of course. You deserve that. However, my part in this was sketchy." Egon closed his eyes in concentration. "Early that afternoon, I received a summons from Ossip. I was not at home, and it was late in the day by the time the message caught up to me. I hastened to his apartments and found him alone."

"Did you pass anyone on the way in?"

"Only Ossip's personal guard, stationed beside the entrance to Ossip's quarters. Your father motioned me to sit, for he was engaged at the computer."

"What was he working on?"

"Frankly, I paid scant attention, but there were columns on the screen, not solid blocks of text."

"Do you remember the background color of the screen?"

"Why?" asked Blackie.

"Mercury Prime's computer system is color coded.

A red screen deals with weapons systems, yellow with banking, green with commerce, and so on."

"It may have been yellow," said Egon. "No, wait! Amber."

"Amber screens are security files," said Kemal. It was probable that his father, concerned over his position, had been coding his computer clone. "The computer will accept an amber command only from a family member."

"Then Ossip must have been working on internal files," said Egon.

"The question that remains is whether he was working on a file of his own or someone else's."

"You said they were security locked. How could he have accessed another person's files?" demanded Blackie.

"It's not easy, but it can be done. He didn't try to hide the file from you?"

Egon shook his head. "Nor did he motion me to look at it. He simply finished his work and turned to me. But you must understand, Kemal. Ossip and I were friends. I was in his confidence."

"And then?"

"Then he gave me this." Egon reached into the neck of his tunic and pulled out a key on a chain. It was made of unremarkable steel, the head a simple trefoil.

"But this must be important."

"No. I have tried to give it to my captors, and they have laughed in my face. They say I am trying to palm off rubbish for a king's ransom."

"Even Gordon? He never overlooks a possibility," said Kemal.

"Gordon did not overlook it, but he found no lock it would fit, nor did he find intelligence in what Ossip told me. He said steel was worth more than gold, and the right man would have the answer."

"That is enigmatic. No wonder you are perplexed. Steel is for steel." Kemal thought on his father's words, but could find no meaning in them. "Did he give you any indication of who the right man was?"

"No."

Kemal studied the old man's face. "Who is it who seeks your life? You said Gordon was not interested."

"That's officially. I don't know who's been responsible for the attempts on my life, but I am sure they are related to Ossip."

"Why?" asked Kemal.

"What other reason could there be?" said Egon. "My imprisonment was related to your father. He is," said Egon ironically, "my only claim to fame. Would it were my music."

"And this!" said Kemal, fingering the key that Egon had handed him.

"It is yours if you want it. I only kept it as a memento of my friend."

Kemal's hand closed over the piece of steel. "Thank you. I hope my visit won't bring you trouble."

"Life is danger," replied Egon. "Visit me again if you are near. We will speak of your past and what more I can recall of your father."

"I would like that," said Kemal.

Blackie frowned. "You won't come back," she said.

"Since when can you read my mind? I don't recall you did a particularly good job of it earlier," said Kemal dryly.

A hint of color showed under Blackie's white skin.

"And," Kemal continued, "I resent being lumped in with the general run."

"And I resent being ignored," said Blackie.

"When you do something worth notice, you will be sure to get it," returned Kemal. He turned to Egon. "How did such an even-tempered, generous man befriend such a contrary child?"

"She reminds me of my wife, who died many years ago."

Kemal regarded the Musician with increased respect. "You are a brave man," he said.

Egon smiled. "Luckier than most. Most men only dream of the devotion and passion that were mine."

"You are treating me as if I do not exist!" said Blackie.

Kemal put on a contrite face. "You are right," he said. "I apologize."

Egon's smile faded. "You will try to find a lock for that key?"

"Yes."

"You could wear out your life looking and never find it—any more than you may find your father's killer," said the Musician.

"I know."

"Ossip is dead. Let him rest." Egon's words were gentle.

"I wish I could," said Kemal. "I barely remember my father, Egon, but he haunts me." He thought ironically that his words were doubly true. His father's hologram materialized in his mind's eye. "In most people's eyes, he seems to have been a good man. I fear his killer has profited from his death these many years."

Egon's eyes grew misty. "He was a good man. Especially within the context of Mercury and the heritage of the Sun Kings. Great wealth presents many temptations, many opportunities to place oneself above other men. Ossip did not do that. I would like to see his killer punished."

"I will do my best," said Kemal. "As much for my spirit as his."

Chapter Twenty-three

Dalton Gavilan, at the head of a detachment of Mercurian fighters, sailed toward Tortuga. They would reach the station about an hour after Kemal's rendezvous. Dalton did not wish to threaten the exchange, but he did not intend to be far away should the prototype fall into danger.

His communications link beeped, and the blue light above it winked, indicating a scrambled transmission. He waited for the light to go off, then cut in his communications line.

"This is Gordon."

"Yes, Father."

When his father used his name to identify himself,

Dalton had learned not to reply formally.

"I've received word from a source on Tortuga that Ardala's representative did not appear. Moreover, the same source tells me Ardala herself left the station more than twenty-four hours ago," said Gordon.

"Then where's Kemal?"

"My source saw him leave the Black Pennon cafe . . . forty-three minutes ago.

"I'm going in." Dalton could not keep the eagerness from his voice.

"Dalton."

The warning note in his father's voice stopped Dalton's impulsive hand as he reached for the throttle. "Sir."

"Remember what I taught you. Don't assume. The delay could be legitimate. Kemal might even be in danger." Gordon's cautionary words were mirrored in his tone.

Dalton snorted contemptuously. The sound was reminiscent of a bull preparing to charge.

"Get the facts," said Gordon. "Better yet, get the laser."

"And if Kemal has betrayed us?"

"Tortuga is not a large station. I have no doubt you could find a man with a healthy price on his head there." Gordon could not see his son's smile, but he knew it was there.

Gordon cut the transmission, and Dalton opened a clear line to his squad. "This is Solar Flare," he said. "Lock in course now in transmission. Report."

"Flash One, course accepted."

"Flash Two, locked in."

"Flash Three, course accepted."

The answers came as quick as the seconds, and
Dalton eased his throttle forward. "Fall in," he ordered. "One-third power."

The detachment tightened formation, two ships
taking up positions on either of Dalton's wings, the
third flying pickup. They arced in a soft turn and
headed for the point on the charts that signified
Tortuga.

O O O O O

Kemal sent his ship away from Tortuga in a burst
of his docking jets, curving around the space station
to clear space where he could set a trajectory for Mercury. As he passed the station's sphere of influence,
he heard his cousin Dalton request docking coordinates. He punched the identification code for the
standard Mercurian fighter into his computer and
hit the search function. Four of the blue dots on his
sensor screen turned red. Their military formation
further confirmed his identification.

Kemal altered his course and pushed the throttle
forward. His ship screamed through a turn that put
him on a parallel course to his cousin, but toward
Mercury, not Tortuga. He cut his communications
link into Mercury's combat frequency, knowing
Dalton always monitored that line, by computer, if
not directly, and that a call would certainly get
through. "Dalton, you're going the wrong way!"

"Kemal!" Dalton's grim voice was surprised.

"Yes, Kemal. Who else?"

Kemal's sensors showed Dalton's squad in a flip
turn as they whirled to follow him.

"Father sent me to make inquiries. We were becoming concerned."

Kemal grinned at Dalton's bland explanation of his presence. "He should be. We've been double-crossed. Ardala's messenger never came. Neither did the laser. The Gavilan name has been dishonored," he said pompously.

"Ardala will pay for this," said Dalton. He flipped his ship over once more, heading back to Tortuga. His squad followed blindly. Dalton charged the station, his speed blinding. He was still inside the station's defenses, cleared for the area, and Tortuga's defense system did not react to his charge quickly enough. He skimmed the station, sending a zinging series of laser bolts into Ardala's space dock. His squad followed suit, burning the dock to twisted fragments. Tortuga's defenses blasted ineffectually as Dalton streaked out of range.

Kemal grinned at Dalton's impetuosity, but his stomach was still in a nervous clutch. Until he could look into Gordon Gavilan's eyes and see his uncle's heart, he would not know his fate. He flew his ship ruthlessly, wanting to face the inevitable and deal with it. Far ahead, the blazing face of the Sun beckoned him home.

○ ○ ○ ○ ○

Duernie braced against the bales of gossamer, clinging like a monkey to the plaited cable that secured them. Gossamer was stacked in one- by two-yard cubes, wrapped in brown burlap, and coated with protective film. The bales were then tied with cable and a hook loop fixed to the six cube crossover points. The loops were then used to lash the bales into lots, and to load them. Duernie was balanced between the bales in a loosely secured lot.

"Got it, Oz?" The voice of a dock worker sounded in her ear.

"Yup. Oh, no."

The bundle lurched as the loading hook slipped, and the lot thumped to the floor of Tir Plantia Warren spacedock. Duernie clung to the ropes, praying that she would not be knocked off.

"Come back, Oz. I got it," said the first man, catching the hook a second time. He slipped it into the loop, tested it, and gave Oz a double thumbs-up.

"Clear, Dave!" yelled Oz, and his companion jumped back from the bales.

Once again the lot began to rise, and Duernie knew the next few moments were crucial. She was not invisible. If a dockhand were standing directly below the load, he might notice her.

Dave watched the lot rise, shoving his white hard hat back on his head. He put his hands on his hips as he watched the load. Suddenly, he began to gesture frantically.

Oz, intent on moving the lot onto the transport, did not see him at first. Dave put his hands to his mouth in a makeshift megaphone.

"It's slipping!" he bellowed. "Watch it! It's slipping!"

His words were barely audible over the noise of the loading crane, but Oz, conditioned by years of experience, heard him. He slowed the crane, which now had the lot suspended over the cargo pad of the transport.

The lot jerked on the hook, half of it dropping a quarter of a yard as the knots gave.

Duernie could not repress a yelp. Luckily, the crane's powerful motor covered it. The shift in the load dragged at her left arm, and she knew she was going to have to get a new grip, or she would be pulled apart, despite the fact that she was suspended sixty feet in the air, with a surface of solid metal beneath her. She set her eyes on her new handhold, took a fresh grip with her right hand, and reached for it. She caught the rope near the top of a bale and heard the load creak ominously.

Her new position brought her head above the lowered half of the lot, and she ducked down, hoping she was out of Oz's sight.

"It's stabilized!" yelled Dave. He motioned for Oz to proceed.

Duernie felt the crane begin to move, and she held her breath, lest the load disintegrate under her. She kept her eyes on the cargo pad, counting off the seconds as it rose to meet her.

"It's holding!" shouted Dave. "Set it down!"

Oz, from his throne on top of the crane, nodded. He directed the metal arm to deposit its burden. The crane dipped into the transport's cargo hold, and the lot disappeared.

Once again, Duernie was almost knocked from her perch as the load hit the floor in an uneven bump, but this time there was solid ground beneath her feet. The minute the lot settled, she dropped her handholds and sank to the floor, crouching at the center of the bale so that her back was the only thing visible from above.

She felt the bales give as someone climbed on them, and the lack of strain as a crewman unhooked the loop. The bales gave again as he climbed down from his perch. Duernie's heart was pounding so hard that she was sure he could hear it. She heard footsteps on the metal deck, and she breathed for the first time in seconds.

With knowledge of momentary safety came anger. She had paid far too much for this passage. When she returned to Tir Plantia, she vowed to exact retribution from her hooded contact. Her frown was deep as she wedged herself into a more comfortable position and prepared to wait for launch.

Chapter Twenty-four

Killer Kane had Mercury in his sights. It was a black ball against the brilliant background of the Sun, a dot on his viewscreen, but he knew it might as well have been a black pearl for the wealth it represented. Kane was not impressed by wealth, but he was impressed by power. Money, or its equivalent in merchandise, was just one road to power. He had made sure of his own wealth when he agreed to work for RAM, and he had been building a financial empire ever since. He itched to get his hands on some of the money the Gavilans used so freely.

"This is Thug One," said Kane into his communications link. "We are six minutes, twenty-one seconds from target. We're going in fast—we're hitting fast. We have to go down, and we'll need all the time we can muster. We're sure to have the Gavilans on our tails, in spite of our stealth capabilities. If Dalton Gavilan gets us on visual, he won't let go."

"I copy," replied Poxon.

"Thug Three?" asked Kane.

"I copy," said Malone.

"You don't sound happy," said Kane.

"I wouldn't've signed on if I'd known you were gonna hit the Gavilans."

"You did sign on. You know the choices."

"I'd rather take my chances with Dalton Gavilan than you," said Malone. "I'll stick."

"Good." Kane made the single unobtrusive word a possibility of the most drastic evil. "Stay tight. Keep your eyes open. We should be able to evade Mercury's automatic defenses with our electronic systems, but you never know what new toys the Gavilans have bought. We're going to do our best to stay away from Mercury Prime. Ready for weapons check?"

"Affirmative," replied Poxon.

"Yup," said Malone.

"Missiles?"

Poxon flipped through his checklist. "All go—all strapped down tight."

"Thug Three?" asked Kane.

"Missiles in place. All secure," said Malone.

"Forward lasers?" asked Kane.

"Check."

"Check."

Kane ticked off each piece of armament in turn.

"Weapons check confirmed," he said at last. "Course two-seven-one point four-three. Stick to me."

The *Rogue* turned to a new trajectory, its wingmen following like smaller shadows. The flying wedge charged toward Mercury in headlong flight, their stealth systems fully operational. By monitoring general communications from the planet, Kane had located Mercury Prime. His course brought the wing in to Mercury on the opposite side of the planet, but he knew he would have to flirt with Mercury Prime in order to hit the crystal farm.

He pulled up the coordinates Ardala had given him and fed them into his astrogational system. The computer plotted a course from the trajectory he flew. Kane keyed in the code for Mercury Prime and hit a button marked "evade." The numbers on the course readout blipped, and the computer offered him a new course. This one took him to the security satellite that Ardala's information placed in orbit above the crystal farm, then into the farm itself on one set of co-ordinates, but gave him an escape route away from Mercury Prime. Kane's green eyes warmed with satisfaction, like green seas on a summer day. He fed the information into his automatic astrogation function, setting it up so that he could make his escape with the punch of a button.

The black ball of Mercury grew in his viewscreen, lightening as he neared it. The Sun receded behind the little planet as Kane closed on it, until there was a halo of sunlight backing Mercury in reflected glory. As they closed on the planet, Kane's astrocomputer pulled up a readout of satellites and shipping around Mercury, routing the *Rogue* through it all. The Mariposas appeared as an artificial ring around the planet. One of them was masquerading, hiding its function as a guard for the Dancers' crystals under the innocent configuration of a Mariposa solar satellite. With the information Ardala had given him, Kane would not be fooled by the resemblance.

He checked the ships in the area, and, besides the usual busy commercial traffic, he found only one detachment of military craft, flying sweeps over their homeland at regular intervals. They were operating, as was customary for the Gavilans, in pairs, and the wing consisted of six pairs. "Watch it, now," said Kane softly.

"I see 'em," responded Malone. "I'm stayin' right with you."

"On course," said Poxon shortly.

Kane angled toward Mercury, cutting a fine line between the Mariposas and the flight paths of the reconnaissance craft. He saw one pair vanish over the horizon. His computer told him another pair would not be in sight for four minutes. Kane went in.

He sent his ship toward the bracelet the Mariposas made around the planet, and his astrogational computer read each satellite as it came into range. It discarded the first three, then locked on to the fourth. "Identification code confirmed" flashed in solid red block letters across the screen. Kane dove at the satellite, his wing close behind. As the satellite grew on his screen, he activated his first two missiles, then pulled up his targeting computer. True to Ardala's coordinates, the computer locked on target. Kane, with a rakish smile under his slim black mustache, fired the missiles, pulling his ship up as he did so.

Poxon and Malone followed suit. As they veered away from the satellite, the first missile struck, sending up a shower of golden fragments as it destroyed the cylinder attached like a cocoon to the body of the satellite and one of its flaring butterfly wings.

He cut under the orbit of the Mariposas, heading for the surface in a dive that was as dangerous as it was dramatic, but Kane did not want to lose a second. He wanted to be skimming the ground by the time the next flight came by. If he could cut close enough to the surface, his automatic camouflage system would make it nearly impossible to detect him beyond visual range.

His men followed him down, clinging grimly to his wings. They knew Kane's methods. Sometimes he took risks, but the rewards of flying with him were substantial. He made sure he paid full price, and with Kane there was another advantage. Mercenaries became used to working for people who wanted a bloody piece of business done but did not want to get their hands dirty. That was why they hired someone to do the job. Mercenaries were expendable, people one did not admit knowing, no matter how much of one's income was lavished on them.

Kane was a part of the action. He asked no man to do what he would not. When he hired help, that was what he wanted: help. He led his operations personally, and he always picked the most dangerous, dirtiest jobs for himself. Moreover, he was a consummate warrior. The men he hired respected him before they met him. He was one of the hottest rocketjocks in the system, and a dead shot. He was a wizard with a mono knife, and he kept himself in superb condition.

The three ships skimmed the surface of the planet and flew through the darkness with the perfect security of efficient technology. Their passage riffled the sand in a herringbone pattern.

"Coming up on target coordinates," said Kane. "Prepare to launch missiles. You each have your targets."

Poxon clicked the switch on his third missile, releasing it for launch. His finger hovered over the launch button. "Launch ready," he replied.

"Got it," said Malone, fingers braced against the control panel, his thumb resting lightly on the red button.

"In five," said Kane. "Four, three, two . . . one. Missiles away." He pushed his own launch button.

Three preprogrammed missiles shot from beneath the starboard wing of each ship. They outdistanced the fighters in seconds, disappearing in a trail of white.

"Second flight," ordered Kane. "Ready. Now."

A second set of missiles launched, and Kane sent a third after those. The first flight had found their target, and Kane's sensors showed the impact. "The computer shows a direct hit, right on coordinates," said Kane. "It looks like we've got it."

"Second hit confirmed," said Poxon.

"All right. We're going in. Remember," said Kane. "So far, they can't see us, but, sure as a knife-blade cuts, they can see those missile trails and the explosions. We've got fifteen minutes at best."

The three ships turned, sweeping around in an exhibition arc. Ahead of them was a cloud of mushrooming smoke, white puffs undercut by flame, and laced with fine trails of black. As they watched, the smoke belched, and a pink column shot with sparks blew upward.

"Hit the generator!" crowed Malone.

"That's not where it's supposed to be," said Kane. "If that was the generator, there won't be anything left to raid. Let's take a look. Cut speed one-third."

The three ships slowed, then rose to overfly their target. Without atmosphere, they could make dramatic changes at short notice. They shot over the site.

Kane checked his sensors. They showed damage at the coordinates Ardala had given him, but they also registered a major explosion near the center of the complex and smaller, chain-reaction explosions tracking across the clear space between the original strikes and the central disturbance. Kane's devil-may-care face was strained with anger. He saw his prize melting before his eyes, and he blamed Ardala and her faulty information.

"Sensors can't penetrate this residue," he said. "We're going over again, trying to pick up visual."

The wing reversed its course, and Kane took the ships back, running them at a different angle. The ships' passage helped clear the debris. It now rose in more isolated columns, with the occasional mushroom of a secondary blast. Kane came in as low as he dared, his infrared viewscreen on full.

Beneath him was a ruined dome. One or two large chunks of the roof were still discernable, but most of it had been blown to fragments. The four strike sites smoldered. The center of the dome was a burned-out hole. In the less damaged area between the two, fragments of metal lay like twisted bodies.

"My sensors count no bodies." Poxon's voice was blank.

"I copy, Thug Two," replied Kane.

"That doesn't sound right for a crystal farm," said Malone.

"No," said Kane, contemplative.

"We goin' in?" asked Malone bluntly.

"One more pass," said Kane, sending the *Rogue* around.

Malone and Poxon followed, but Malone said, "We ain't got time for much more. I got a swarm at two o'clock. We got maybe seven minutes."

Kane did not reply. He sent his wicked crimson ship over the strike again, more to confirm his suspicions than anything else. "All right," he said tersely, "Let's get out of here."

"I'm with you, boss." Under other circumstances, the relief in Malone's voice would have made Kane smile.

"Thugs One and Two, cut in automatic course coordinates," said Kane.

"I copy," replied Poxon smoothly.

"Done!" replied Malone.

"That wasn't a crystal farm," said Poxon.

"Affirmative, Thug Two," said Kane. "Nor were those the coordinates to knock out a security system."

"What'd we hit?" asked Malone, curious.

"The generators. Knowing the basic construction of those old domes, I'd guess it had two generators on full power, the other two as back-up units. I'll wager our first strike hit the main power source, the second the other two."

"And the third?" asked Poxon.

"That, Thug Two, is interesting. I think we just did some free work, and I don't like it. Whatever we blew up, it was big. I am looking forward to studying the photographs on it."

"You mean we hit the wrong target?"

"In a matter of speaking," said Kane. "We hit the target we were told to hit. It just didn't happen to be a crystal farm, and the coordinates we were given blew the whole thing. My guess is we blew up a refinery."

The import of Kane's words was slowly penetrating Malone's mental processes. "You mean you was tricked?" he asked.

Anger flashed through Killer Kane's face and centered in his eyes, turning them to green lasers. "Yes." He did not relish being used, and he intended to extract vengeance for the humiliation, the loss of funds, and the risk.

"By Ardala?" There was amazement in Malone's answer. He was not tactful, but his reactions were honest.

"I do not know," said Kane tightly. "The possibility exists. The possibility also exists that she was given false information. I will find out."

Both Poxon and Malone knew Kane's tone, though they had never heard it before. It was a cold determination that would let nothing stand in its way. They knew, without a shadow of a doubt, that Kane would extract payment from the person who had used him.

The planet skimmed by beneath them as the three renegades shot toward a clear exit trajectory. The craters were blemishes on the face of the planet.

They overflew a track city like hunting hawks. Far ahead lay Phidias Warren and their escape trajectory.

"What's that?" asked Poxon suddenly.

"Specify, Thug Two," replied Kane.

"Point alpha-beta-X on your sensors," said Poxon.

"I see it," said Kane. Their flight path took them within a hundred yards of the point. Kane strained his eyes and was rewarded by the sight of a new survival dome arching above the rocks. It glowed an enticing red on the infrared viewscreen. "Let's find out," said Kane suddenly, and dove for the dome.

Chapter Twenty-five

Kane's detachment streaked over the Mercurian landscape, intent on escape. The Mercurian patrol followed, trying desperately to hang on to the swifter craft.

"We're losing them, Messenger Leader. They've got more power than we do," said the patrol's wingman, Messenger One.

The wing leader lost no time in passing the buck once the situation had become grave. "Plot a course from their present trajectory. I'm calling in," he said. "This is Messenger Leader, code red. We have a renegade. I say again, we have a renegade."

"This is Mercury Prime. Confirm code red."

"I say again, code red!" snapped the patrol leader.

Code red meant a breach of Mercurian security. It authorized direct communications with Gordon Gavilan.

"This is Gordon Gavilan." Gordon's voice was a snarl of rage. "Report!" he demanded.

"We have visual contact with three ships. We are overflying power station . . ." The pilot paused as he consulted his maps. ". . . Alpha six-three-one. It is destroyed. Ships running away from us."

"Stay with them!" ordered Gordon, his face florid with anger, his voice like a rasp. This was the second report of destruction he had had in as many minutes, though the loss of an automated power station on the surface was not a fourth as painful as the destruction of his secret laboratory and the nearly completed giant laser.

The Mercurian security wing watched as Kane left the planet's surface in a power drive that put his ship on a perfect ninety-degree trajectory.

"Catch that course change!" said Messenger Leader.

"Change logged," replied Messenger One.

"Good." The wing leader turned his attention back to his communications link. "Request backup. Renegade flying trajectory estimated at oh-five-four high."

"We copy, Messenger Leader. We've got him in our sights. He's—gone!" said the wing leader of another squad.

"Did you sight the assailants?" asked the Sun King, his question nearly a shout. His rage was congealing into cold fury.

"Yes, sir. We had three red fighters, no serial numbers or identifying marks, except that the first was larger than the second and third and carried geometric decoration. They're chain lightning. They pulled away from us as if we were docked."

Gordon Gavilan whirled away from the communications station, his hands coming down on the keys to the main system. He punched in the emergency code himself. It took exactly seven seconds for the link to go through. When the computer showed him an active line, Gordon proceeded with no more ceremony. "Dalton, this is your father," he snarled. "There's been a strike on the laboratory. I want them, Dalton! And they've apparently got the newest in stealth capabilities, because we can't find them on the scope, and a squad leader had them in sight seconds ago. Do you copy?"

"I copy," replied Dalton.

"Get him for me, Dalton." Gordon's words were icy.

"Affirmative," replied Dalton. He adjusted his course, once again, to follow Kemal. Although Kemal had not said a word, he had immediately altered course to coincide with the coordinates Messenger Leader had provided. Once again, Dalton was trailing his cousin.

"See anything?" asked Kemal as they neared the coordinates.

"Nothing," responded Dalton. "Nothing on visual, either."

Kemal cut his communications link into the private line that Gordon was using. Any family member had the capability of monitoring internal communications. "This is Kemal," he said. "Was there a visual description of the ships?"

"Yes," replied Gordon. "Kemal?"

"Yes."

"What are you doing here? Where's the laser? Safeguard that first!"

"I'll give you a report later. Right now, I need to know whatever you have on the visual sighting."

"Red," replied Gordon. "Definitely fighters, but not Mercurian. The leader flew a larger ship."

"That makes them illegal," said Kemal.

"Good guess," said Dalton.

The wheels were turning in Kemal's head. "We should be coming up on a trajectory intersection."

Kemal watched his sensors, hoping for a sign that he was close to the hiding place of the attack squad. He strained his eyes into the blackness, trying to pick them out of it.

"Try scanning for heat trails," said Dalton.

"This close to Mercury? With all the traffic we have?" Kemal was incredulous. To pinpoint a vessel by heat trails was difficult at best, next to impossible when sensors had to deal with busy shipping lanes. It was like looking for a needle in a haystack, and they did not have time or energy remaining. Instead, Kemal pulled away.

"Where are you going?" demanded Dalton. "Answer me!"

"To tail him," said Kemal. He set his course to match the fleeing ships' escape trajectory and ran at full throttle. His energy gauge registered one-eighth full. He had to find the intruders quickly, or he would run out of energy. Because his sensors registered nothing, he risked overflying his quarry, and a spectacular collision. He peered into the darkness. Far away there was a brief flash of light, like sunlight on a ship's hull.

"Kemal, you fool! You're going to get yourself killed!"

Kemal smiled at Dalton's warning, knowing that Dalton was not worried for his safety, but for incurring his father's anger. Gordon would want the thieves, not a net full of space trash.

Kemal dove forward, searching black space. There had been a time, in the early history of flight, when a man's eyes made the difference between life and death. With the advent of radar and progressively more sophisticated sensor systems, that physical prowess had become obsolete. Now, at the other end of technology, they were back to square one.

Kemal knew it took more than good eyes to find a craft in the void. It took a knowledge of how sunlight reflected off metal, or plasti, catching a nuance of motion in the dark. Kemal's vision was good, but like most twenty-fifth century pilots, he had not been taught to rely on it. He thought of his friend Buck Rogers, and of Rogers's straightforward approach to a problem. Kemal tried to emulate him now, scanning space for the intruders. He peered into the void, his eyes on the point where he had seen light.

"You want to spot fire," Buck had once told him, "get a sighting on the enemy's muzzle flashes, and keep your eyes on it. Don't take them off for a minute. If you're persistent, you'll be able to locate him."

Kemal followed that advice now. His patience was rewarded. The ships ahead of him turned, and for a good thirty seconds, the Sun caught them broadside,

illuminating their sleek cylindrical bodies. Kemal
studied them, and his mouth dropped open in surprise. He had seen the lead ship before, and he knew
it was flown by the greatest rogue in the solar
system.

"Kemal, report!"

Dalton's voice grated out of Kemal's communications link. He ignored it. Instead, he matched the detachment's movements, pursuing them recklessly,
his energy dangerously low.

"Kemal, what have you got?"

Kemal took pity on his cousin.

"I've got the attack squad on visual."

"Then fire on them!"

"With what?" asked Kemal. "We don't have a gyro
or missile that can track a full-stealth craft. I'd need
to get within laser range and fire by sight—and that's
not going to happen."

"Why not?" demanded Dalton.

"Because those ships are about one-third faster
than this welder's nightmare I'm flying. I can't get in
range, and I'm out of fusion material."

"What's their course heading?"

Kemal relayed it.

"I plot that as a direct course to Mars."

"Sure," said Kemal. "Are you willing to bet they
don't end up there?"

Dalton said nothing. He was grasping at straws.
He knew as well as Kemal that a favorite pirate trick
was to run away from the scene of pillage on one
course, then change dramatically, ending up somewhere completely different.

"You might as well come in," said Dalton.

"I know," answered Kemal, "but I keep hoping I'll get close enough for a good camera shot."

"Can you identify the craft?" asked his cousin.

"I am very much afraid so," replied Kemal. "And it is not an answer you—or Uncle Gordon, for that matter—will like."

Dalton said nothing. If Kemal could identify the ship, then there was every likelihood that he had encountered it in his work with NEO. His ability to identify the vessel might be the beginning of a case for disloyalty. If Dalton proceeded with care, Kemal might find himself in exile . . . permanently. In spite of the gravity of the situation, a smug smile bloomed on Dalton's grim lips.

Ahead of Kemal, the black ship made a final abrupt turn. The Sun caught its upswept tail and slim wings, like fins, as it turned away and dove into the sea of blackness that was space.

Chapter Twenty-six

Kane."

Gordon Gavilan pronounced the name with a flat acceptance that made the hairs rise on the back of Kemal's neck. Kemal watched the severe lines on either side of his uncle's mouth deepen. "Yes," he said.

The communications alarm over Gordon's desk blared like a siren. It was reserved for emergencies, and Gordon jumped for his communications link. "What is it?" he barked.

"Sir, I am picking up an urgent communique from Ubrahil Carrera to Phidias Warren security."

"Now," said Gordon, and Carrera's breathless voice

flared out of the link.

". . . devastated! Broken to pieces! It will take months to rebuild. I have three men dead! Dead!" Carrera was hysterical.

Gordon listened coldly to the transmission.

"Get hold of yourself," said the impersonal voice of Phidias Warren's dispatcher. "Tell me what happened."

"What happened? We were hit!" Carrera's words tumbled over each other. "Blasted as if we were a military target!"

"By whom?" asked the dispatcher, his flat voice a ploy to calm Carrera's panic.

"Kane!" said Carrera. "Killer Kane, here on Mercury! What do you make of that?"

"Tell me," said the dispatcher, "in simple words, exactly what happened." The dispatcher's refusal to be upset was soothing, and Carrera gathered the threads of his story together.

"We were in the middle of testing a new filtering system we hoped would produce more uniform crystals, when there was a dull boom, like someone dropped an empty nuclear fuel drum. Then the power died." Carrera cleared his throat.

"Go on," said Gordon grimly.

"We got the emergency systems going just about the time the air started to foul. The lights came up at half power, and standing in our midst was a man dressed in a plain black spacesuit. He had eyes that burned like green crystals, and he carried a needle gun. Before I could open my mouth to protest, he motioned his companions toward the vats. Two of my men tried to stop them, and he shot them! Shot them down like vermin! Shot them down at my feet!" His voice rose.

The grim set of Gordon's mouth hardened as he listened.

"Then what?" demanded the dispatcher, bringing Carrera under control.

"One of the other men knocked poor Andiep to the ground. He was old and could not stand the shock. He died there on the floor, the rest of us afraid to make a move to help him. The robbers threw the smaller crystals into a burlap sack—with no regard or care, mind you. When they had gathered all the crystals that were near harvesting, the man with the gun turned it on the vats and trays."

"Go on." The dispatcher's cold prodding was drawing out Carrera's story.

"He destroyed everything! Everything broken, useless!"

"Did he damage the power couplings or the generators, or breach the dome?"

"What?" asked Carrera. "No. Why should he? It will take us weeks to recover, months to develop the crystals we had. And the deaths? What about the deaths? Is that man to be allowed to walk away from this?"

"How did you know you were facing Killer Kane?" asked the dispatcher.

"He told me!" said Carrera.

"Tell me what he said."

"He said," Carrera almost shouted, "that he did not have time to be civil, and he would shoot anyone who resisted him. I demanded to know the meaning of his intrusion, and he stared me down with those uncanny green eyes and said one word: 'Theft.' "

"Then he told you he was Kane."

"No, no, no! Then he demanded all our crystals. I asked him who he thought he was, and he replied, 'Kane.' "

"Carrera."

"Yes?" The businessman's reply was acid.

"You can rest assured Kane will pay for this—sooner or later." The dispatcher uttered the placebo calmly.

"Yes," repeated Carrera starkly. "The Dancers will see to it."

The transmission clicked as he disengaged, claiming the last word.

"There can be no peace." The light in Gordon Gavilan's eyes was dead. Even his son Dalton had not heard such emptiness in his voice. The flesh of his face sagged like an old man's. He faced the ruin of all his dreams, and he feared the ruin of Mercury.

That Killer Kane, a renegade mercenary, had been able to breach Mercury's extensive defenses confirmed his worst fears. He saw the planet defenseless in the face of a world gone mad with power. He saw his family wealth crumbling like brittle clay.

Though he had no love for Gordon, Kemal did not enjoy watching his disintegration. "You are right," he said. "This has been an evil day for Mercury, but setbacks do not mean defeat."

Gordon turned to his desk and punched the security alarm. There were armed guards at his side in moments.

Dalton, from his chair behind Kemal, stirred. "Don't you think that's a little extreme?" he asked.

Gordon glared at his son. "You're awake?"

"I am always awake."

"One would never know it," said Gordon acidly.

Dalton shifted his broad shoulders. "There was nothing to say."

"And now?" snarled his father, his anger beginning to seep through his control.

"Now, I think we have been insulted. I do not like it."

Gordon began to pace the floor of his office, his broad feet hard on the white stone. "Kane went through our defenses as if they did not exist. If he can do it, others can."

"No." Kemal's interjection brought Gordon to a halt. "Kane is a specialist. He has expended a large percentage of his resources on his ship. His stealth systems are not cost effective for an armada, and, once warned, they can be broken."

Dalton cocked an ironic eye at his cousin. "Your vast areas of expertise never cease to amaze me."

"It doesn't take an expert to know chaff blasters will make any ship show up like a cardboard cutout. If we armed all the Mariposas, we could surround Mercury with a rain of chaff. Kane and his men would never have gotten away."

Gordon was nodding. "Old-fashioned," he said. "So old-fashioned that we deactivated them. I think there are units still in place on half of the Mariposas." Energy was growing in his footsteps. "We will reset our defenses, and we will rebuild."

"There is one thing more," said Kemal.

"Kane is a mercenary," commented Dalton.

"Yes. He seldom works unless he has an employer.

To raid Mercury under our noses was a high-cost operation, and he had help. Who would be willing to risk so much money, and for what?"

"Kane and Ardala Valmar are known associates," said Dalton.

Kemal blessed Dalton for making his job easy. "They have been known to work together," he agreed. "And Ardala betrayed Mercury on Tortuga."

"I think," said Gordon slowly, "that I am going to have a chat with the lovely Miss Valmar."

Kemal and Dalton looked at one another, for despite the courtesy of the words, Gordon's statement was fraught with intimations of retribution.

O O O O O

Duernie woke with a start. Her foot slipped off a bale of gossamer as the lot she was hiding inside was lifted from the transport deck, again by crane. She scrabbled for a handhold, her eyes still full of gritty sleep. Not able to use a hand, she blinked rapidly to clear them and clung to the bale ropes for dear life.

She could see the transport floor receding, and she knew she was being lifted out of the transport and onto the loading docks of Mercury Prime. The knowledge sent a thrill through her. It pumped a rush of adrenaline into her system, and the last vestiges of sleep faded away.

"For pete's sake, Jock! Pull it up straight, or not at all!"

The dock foreman yelled orders at his crane operator, who, fortunately for the cargo, ignored his superior.

Duernie felt herself swinging fifty yards above the ground, and her grip was tiring. She tried to adjust her hold but only succeeded in nearly losing it. The lot swayed at the end of the crane's hook.

"Load shift! Load shift!" bawled the foreman.

"I see it," Jock muttered, counterbalancing the load's sway. Once stabilized, he swung it over the side of the transport and onto the deck, near another lot of cloth.

A dockhand released the loading hook, and Jock took his crane in for another load, but Duernie, solid deck beneath her feet once more, sagged. She had been in some tight spots, but never had she been more frightened. She relaxed at the center of the bales of cloth, her eyes closed, her body like jelly. Relief drained her strength. Her joints would not hold her weight. She leaned into a bale and closed her eyes, drinking in the spicy scent of the perfumed cloth. Her eyes flew open as footsteps approached her hiding place.

"You been keepin' up with the news?" she heard a voice ask.

"Naw. I depend on you to do that." A second voice chuckled.

"Murray, you were lazy even when we were in school."

"At least I wasn't the class brainchild," said Murray. "What news is there?"

"Don't tell anybody I said so, but the Gavilan laser is gone."

"Gone! Stolen?"

"No. Destroyed. Seems three ships got in under our defenses and blew us up . . ."

The words that followed were unintelligible to Duernie. The meaning of those she'd heard, though, was not. She was glad that the Gavilans had suffered a loss. She intended for them to suffer much more.

She checked the time and realized that it would be six hours before she dared to venture out of her make-shift apartment. Only during Mercury Prime's down shift were there fewer than three people on the docks.

As she settled down to wait, she caught isolated scraps of information: a name here, a place there. The mention of Kemal brought a rush of angry tears to her eyes. She wiped them away with the back of one brown hand.

Kemal was a traitor. The logic of her thought was comforting. Unfortunately, it failed to affect her heart. That rebellious organ thumped away stubbornly, refusing to erase Kemal's image. She knew handsomer men, but Kemal's brown attractiveness suited her, satisfied her desert-bred soul. He was restrained, both in demeanor and in appearance, not given to wild excesses, though he could imitate a solar storm easily enough. She loved the contrast of war and peace that played their scenarios across Kemal's soul.

Another lot of gossamer thumped down next to her. A bale weighed close to two hundred pounds. The lots were more than three tons of merchandise. She scrunched down inside her hiding place, trying to make sure she was clear should the crane operator drop another bundle.

Once she escaped the bales of cloth, she had to find an isolated computer terminal, one that saw little or no action. She had devised a plan for trying to milk

the security system of its identity codes. Once into
the computer, the identity codes would make it possible to overload the Mariposas.

She had spent hours working out the electronic details, and there would be no margin for error.

"How I am looking forward to this," she murmured.
"Kemal Gavilan, this will be the back of my hand!
You are scum, and I will not dignify you with more
notice. But I will take your precious moneymakers
and blast them out of the sky. Then we will see who is
the winner."

The cargo docks of Mercury Prime echoed with the
various sounds of commerce. Duernie's whisper was
lost among them.

Chapter Twenty-seven

Kemal left his uncle, feeling drained. He sought the relative security of his quarters. He was bone tired. He had accomplished his purpose, and so far he had survived, but he felt no sense of achievement, only fatigue.

He bore the Gavilan name, but he was no real part of the power structure. He was an annoyance to Gordon and a rival to Dalton. He knew they both wished him dead. Of his "loving" family, only Tix held him in the least affection.

He thought of the camaraderie he had enjoyed with NEO. The Martian Wars were the catalyst that had drawn the organization together, but its members had found in each other a family. Buck, Wilma—even that rogue Black Barney—were closer to him than anyone on Mercury . . . except Duernie.

Kemal rubbed his forehead fretfully. He was exhausted. He had a headache, and he did not want to cope with the guilt he felt. Duernie was a symbol of the Dancers. He knew she regarded his betrayal as a personal rejection. The thought was painful, a pain he did not want. He tried to push it away, but Duernie's accusing face, frowning with disapproval, swam in his mind. He reached his room with tears stinging his eyelids.

"I've been waiting for you."

Kemal stopped dead in the open doorway. Ramora was curled up at the head of his bed. She wore a minimal amount of gold net and gossamer. In the soft light, her brown hair flamed with red highlights.

Kemal took one step to the side, leaving the doorway free. "Out!" he said.

She smiled, ignoring the order. She slithered across the bed. "Let me help you relax," she offered.

Kemal regarded her with an anger out of all proportion to her actions. He knew it had to do with her invasion of his privacy. She was an attractive kitten, but she was Gordon's, and therefore dangerous. "Did my uncle send you here?" Kemal asked abruptly.

"No." She pouted at him.

Kemal reached for her hand. "You must leave," he said.

Ramora put her small hand in his, and Kemal pulled her to her feet. She pressed close to him, her hands searching. "You don't really want me to leave," she breathed.

"Yes," replied Kemal. "I do." This was a time his head remained in control. "And Ramora."

She turned, her bearing queenly to cover her feelings.

"Next time, wait for an invitation."

"Gordon always—"

"I am not Gordon," answered Kemal.

"No, you're not!" she said, making the words an insult.

When the door closed behind her, Kemal sank down on the bed. He rolled over and stared at the ceiling, his eyes hollow. He did not for a moment believe Ramora had come on her own. She was one of Gordon's ploys. He wondered how often Dalton had found a similar surprise.

Kemal was surrounded by distrust and greed. They ate into him, trying to make him their own. He wanted to leave them, escape the maze of intrigue and shake the dust of Mercury from his boots. His military training had fostered his love of action, of straight-out combat. He was ill-suited for innuendo and political games. He thought lovingly of the clean, empty reaches of space.

He accepted that darkness and emptiness. It brought a man the simple problem of survival, unhampered by others. He relaxed as the darkness claimed him, sleeping with the intensity of exhaustion.

O O O O O

Gordon Gavilan sat alone in his study, brooding over his losses. Like a wounded tiger, he had repaired to his lair to lick his hurts and gather his forces, waiting for another day. His broad shoulders were hunched, his thick square hands clenched over the arms of his chair like a tiger's extended claws. Like the injured animal, his loss had made him hard-willed. Any semblance of pity was washed away by harsh reality. His dedication to preserving Mercury and the family wealth was now eclipsed by basic personal survival. The strain showed in the nervous tic at the corner of his wide mouth and the dark circles beneath his sunken black eyes.

Gordon had been badly hurt by both Kane's raid and Ardala's treachery. His immediate instinct was to lash out, but his years served him well. He maintained control by an effort of will, but his knuckles were white as he gripped the chair. He would plot and plan in private and act when the moment was in his favor.

"Father."

Dalton's voice in the door sensor was noncommittal, but it surprised his father. Gordon hit the door control on his desk without replying, the blow so forceful that the door jerked before the heavily sculpted metal sank back into the walls. Dalton entered his father's study quietly, with none of his usual whirlwind intensity. He went to the chair beside his father's desk and sat, subdued.

Gordon regarded his son speculatively, his eyes boring into Dalton's heavy, handsome face. Dalton was not in the habit of seeking interviews. "Did you wish to speak to me?" he asked.

Dalton shifted uncomfortably. Of all the Gavilans, he was the least adept at intrigue. Clever and crafty, he knew he was an open book to his father. "There was a possibility we did not discuss."

Gordon waited, his eyes empty black pits.

Dalton cleared his throat and continued. "We could have a traitor."

"Who would that be?" asked Gordon, forcing his son to name his suspicions.

"Kemal."

"Your jealousy speaks." Gordon snarled the words; he was in no mood for the added burden of his son's suspicions.

"I admit, I don't like him, but it's more than personal antipathy. I didn't like his allegiance to NEO, but I like even less his ability to turn his back on them."

"Is it not possible for a man to make a mistake?" asked Gordon sharply, baiting his son.

"Oh, yes." Dalton laid his cards on the table. "Kemal had the opportunity to sell us out to Ardala."

Gordon nodded, conceding the point. "But why?" he asked acidly.

"To sabotage our efforts." Dalton shot a calculating look at his father. He was used to Gordon's sharpness, but it was uncharacteristic for his father to react so abruptly. He noticed Gordon's tic.

"Why?" repeated Gordon.

"For NEO."

Gordon arched an eyebrow. "You just said Kemal had turned his back on NEO!"

"I said it looked that way." Dalton's voice was low, careful.

"And he would sabotage our rule for NEO."

Dalton nodded. "NEO would be happy to have a sympathetic Gavilan at the head of Mercury's government."

"NEO has no interest in us. They are busy trying to rebuild a blasted planet."

"Then perhaps Kemal is working on his own. The laser represented the possibility of power."

"Perhaps," said Gordon. "And perhaps our ground snake is considerably older and more dangerous."

"Ardala?" Dalton's heavy black eyebrow quirked, in imitation of his father.

"Yes."

"It makes sense. She had the prototype. With other lasers and an easy source of crystals destroyed, she could have an exclusive market."

"Not to mention her well-known liaisons with Kane." The discussion was easing the strain around Gordon's eyes. Some facets of the situation were beginning to make sense.

"Very astute," said Dalton. "But beneath words, beneath logic, there is a voice of instinct." Dalton leaned forward and grasped his father's arm with a powerful hand. He ignored the nervous tension that made Gordon's arm quiver in his grasp. "Father, that voice disturbs my dreams."

Gordon looked at his son out of jaded eyes. He ran a hand over his clipped black beard, pulling thoughtfully at one of the silver stripes. "I will respect your instincts, Dalton," he said. "And I will continue to weigh Kemal's words and actions." His eyes glittered feverishly. "Perhaps I have been too quick to accept the obvious."

"I felt it my duty to report to you a matter of security," said Dalton.

"I commend your sense of duty, my son." Gordon's

words were strong, but his voice broke.

Dalton reached out, placing a hand on his father's shoulder. "Father, are you all right?"

Gordon ran a hand fretfully over his hair once more. "Of course," he replied evasively. "Just tired."

Dalton rose slowly, his eyes not meeting his father's. He was afraid Gordon would see his motives. His words had given his father's innate distrust and basic dislike of his brother Ossip's son some ammunition. If he were lucky, there would come a time when Gordon would remove Kemal. Dalton waited for that event with a warm anticipation. He changed the subject. "We have a fourth of the chaff blasters up," he said.

"Good," replied Gordon eagerly. "No one is going to get through undetected again. We have become complacent, Dalton, secure in our power. We cannot afford to be."

"That is why I came," said Dalton simply.

His father nodded, watching him retreat from the room. When the door closed behind Dalton, the Sun King leaned back in his chair and steepled his fingers, the tips pressed so tightly together that they were white. His dark brows drew together as he considered what he meant to do. He looked like a wizard contemplating the powers of the universe, despite the involuntarily jumping muscle in his face. The figure of speech was not abstract, for the miracles Gavilan money could produce were close to magic, and power was Gordon Gavilan's religion.

Finally, he reached out and hit a button on his desk controls. The wall opposite his desk split in the center and two panels of mahogany carved with knots of

wildflowers slid back into the walls, revealing a
twenty-foot computer screen. He hit a key and the
dark screen hummed, burst into a rainbow swirl of
color, and cleared to white. Slowly he punched six
more digits into the system.

He waited a good five minutes before his call was
acknowledged, then two more before Ardala Valmar
answered his summons.

"Yes, Gordon?"

The screen showed Ardala life-size, her voluptuous
charms decoratively displayed. Once again, Gordon
marveled at the superb technique that had preserved
her beauty. She was wearing a peacock-blue bodysuit. It buttoned down the front, and she had left a
good hand's span open to make sure her cleavage was
displayed. The lids of her catlike eyes were painted
brilliant green and peacock blue in a black-bordered
pattern that ran to her eyebrows and curved upward
toward her temples. Her shoulder-length black hair
swept under her chin and fell over her shoulders in a
shining black waterfall. Her lips were stained blood
red.

Gordon had forgotten her impact. He had not spoken to Ardala for some time, and she was even more
stunning than in his vivid memories. "Ardala," he
acknowledged.

"You look older, Gordon."

Gordon had fenced with Ardala often enough to
know her ploys for throwing an adversary off balance. He did not rise to the bait, but he clenched his
fingers. "As must we all, Ardala, except for you. Your
beauty grows with the years." His compliment was
brittle.

She preened like a cat. "And you have developed manners," she said.

"But you have not."

"Dear Gordon," said Ardala, wrapping her mouth around his name as if it were candy. "I never had manners." She stretched out a long blue leg. "I never intend to. They get in the way."

One of Gordon's eyebrows rose. "You have a point."

"Manners are inhibiting," she said. "Although I do enjoy them when they're aimed at me." She squirmed in her dark red leather chair, knowing the effect she created.

"I could flatter you all day long, Ardala, and you would no doubt enjoy it, but that is not why I called."

Ardala's eyes darkened. "I enjoyed your nephew," she said wickedly. "He is much like his father."

Ardala knew all the right buttons to push. Gordon felt a wave of anger wash over him. He knew his skin was white. His mouth was drawn to a tight line, as his frustrated temper flared. "Kemal made a bargain with you," said Gordon coldly. "It was not kept."

"I may not keep my promises," said Ardala in a sharp voice, "but I always keep my bargains."

"Then where is my laser?" snapped Gordon.

Ardala thought fast. She could throw Kemal to the family's ravening fangs, but she did not choose to sacrifice him—yet. She decided to tell the absolute truth. "Your laser was delivered in good faith but was stolen by pirates."

"Then, why," snarled Gordon, his fist slamming onto his desk, "didn't you tell me?"

"I knew you would contact me eventually."

Her cavalier attitude infuriated him, but Gordon

kept his temper. "You know me, Ardala. You might have cost lives." Gordon wanted to shout at her, but he didn't, so his face simply darkened with anger.

She chuckled. The sound was a musical gurgle that was infinitely as pleasing as it was inappropriate. "That would have been entertaining," she said.

"Not to me! The only thing that is going to entertain me is the return of my merchandise."

"I have that under consideration." Her voice hardened.

"Your representative did not meet Kemal on Tortuga." Gordon snapped the accusation like a whip.

"No." Ardala refrained from mentioning that she had sent no one to Tortuga and had no knowledge of such a meeting. Really, sticking to the truth simplified matters.

"Well?" demanded Gordon. He rubbed the corner of his mouth, trying to ease the annoyance of the jumping muscle.

Ardala looked away, giving Gordon her petulant profile. "My men were with the laser," she said stiffly.

Gordon leaped to the conclusion she intended. "You have my sympathies at the loss," he said.

"Really? I could do with some . . . sympathy," she said provocatively.

Gordon said nothing. After all these years, and all he knew of her, he still did not trust his voice.

She was quick to seize the advantage and push it. "We should . . . get together, Gordon. It has been a long time. We could talk over old . . . memories."

"Old times," said Gordon. He remembered the wild passion of his first meeting with Ardala, when he was young and she was no less beautiful but considerably more natural. It had been overwhelming, and he had come back from it convinced he would be the man to unite Martian and Mercurian houses of rule. His romantic illusions were punctured by his father's cold practicality, and he had married a manageable Mercurian woman instead. Now, on the other end of perspective, he was glad not to harbor such a powerhouse in his bosom.

"Old times don't have to be the best," said Ardala. "We could make new times, Gordon."

Gordon thought he detected a wistful note. "What is past is past, Ardala."

"Yes," said Ardala, putting an end to speculation. She knew Gordon would never trust her enough to come to her, and she would never risk her security on Mercury Prime. Politics were an inconvenience she had learned to live with.

"What are you doing about my laser?"

"You are persistent, Gordon. I told you, I am looking into it."

"And that means?"

"I have hired a special investigator."

"I want to know his name."

"No."

"It is my property, Ardala," said Gordon. "I deserve to know."

"I will not have my man's cover jeopardized," she said. "A chance word, a computer blip, and he would be dead."

Gordon had to acknowledge the truth of her words. "All right! But I want to be kept informed of his progress," he said pettishly.

"When I have anything to report, I will let you know. Really, Gordon, you know better than to use that tone with me. It only irritates me, and then you know what happens."

"You become a contrary, spiteful cat," said Gordon.

"Yes," said Ardala sweetly.

"My dear, you are a menace."

"I have always tried to be," she answered. "Really, Gordon. Do you think I would steal from a client, then deal in contraband?"

"Of course," replied Gordon, "if you thought you could get away with it. Remember, Ardala. I want the laser."

"So do I," she said. "I do not like to be trifled with."

Chapter Twenty-eight

Kane."

"Yes, Ardala?"

Kane had let Ardala rot on the audio communications link. He knew it would infuriate her. She liked to see her adversaries, and she depended on her personal charms to sway them. She did not enjoy being thwarted.

"Kane. I want visual, and I want it now!"

"We seem to be having a little trouble in that area," he said.

"Tommyrot! Quit playing games with me."

Kane enjoyed taunting her. "Your beauty is too dazzling, Ardala. I have to protect myself."

Her honey voice crystallized. "If you do not put this transmission on visual in the next ten seconds, I will make you pay."

"Promises, promises," said Kane lightly.

"Kane!"

Kane chuckled. He had not contacted her after the run on Mercury, figuring she owed him for the faulty coordinates. Instead, he made her come to him. Now he was forcing her to beg. It was sweet. "All right, Ardala."

He activated his main screen, and Ardala's angry face appeared. She was as beautiful in a rage, with her black eyes flashing fire, as she was when playing the seductive cat.

"Where have you been?" she demanded.

Kane watched her mouth form the words. "Right here," he answered.

"Well? Where are my crystals?"

"Well." Kane's green eyes became serious. "The coordinates you gave me were wrong. We hit a main generator, blowing some other installation. I do not like being used, Ardala. If you want an assassination, you'll have to pay for it. You owe me."

Ardala's mouth dropped open. For once, she was not calculated, only horribly surprised.

"Surprised?" asked Kane. "Come, now, Ardala. When did anyone ever get the best of you?"

"In the end, never," she said harshly. "The coordinates were bad?"

"Yes. There are pieces of that installation from here to Phidias," he said.

"That sneaking little whelp!"

"Unreliable source?" asked Kane innocently.

"That son of an Earth-born pig!" Ardala whirled in a passion, her hair glittering like jet. "Scheming, superior worm! I cannot believe I allowed that puppy . . . !"

"To what?" asked Kane, rubbing salt into her wounds.

Ardala whirled back to him, her eyes full of a consuming force that would have frightened a lesser man. "I will break him," she said softly.

"No doubt. In the meantime, there is the matter of my payment."

"You would have shared in the profit," she said. "I do not find it unreasonable that you should share the loss."

"But I do." Kane's smile died and his eyes hardened to green jade shot with light. "That little miscalculation could have cost me my life. I don't intend to come away empty-handed."

Ardala's angry eyes narrowed. She pumped sweetness into her voice. "Nothing could replace you, Kane. Certainly not money."

Kane almost laughed. She was really upset. Her manipulations were rarely so transparent. "Are you planning to pay me in kind?" he asked.

Ardala's eyes snapped. Kane was not a man she could not dupe. "What do you want?"

"The plans to that solar lens."

Ardala did not want to make an enemy of Kane, but she didn't want to lose her advantage in the marketplace. She hesitated.

"Of course, I can always make sure the Gavilans know who hired me. They have enough money to reach even you."

"All right." Her lips curved in a superficial smile. She would give him the plans, and they would be intact. Kane would detect missing components instantly. She would not, however, include the calibrations for a giant version. It would take time to plot them. Moreover, without an abundant source of crystals, it would take Kane some time to construct a workable model.

"That was too easy," said Kane, cocking his head. "What's the catch?"

"No catch. This is a loss. They happen." Her eyes misted over with purpose. "That doesn't mean I have to sacrifice assets."

"Not possible," said Kane.

"But it is. I do not want our . . . partnership . . . to suffer because of another man's actions."

"Nor would I," responded Kane. "We have had profitable . . . mergers . . . in the past."

"I look forward to many more," she said, her voice growing husky.

Kane knew the blackness of her soul, knew she cared only for the pleasure and profit she could exact from him, but he did not care. Their relationship was simple, without the complications of emotional involvement. He knew she could kill him, yet he returned to the voluptuous vigor of her body and seductive creativity of her mind. "We have been too long apart," he said. "The plans?"

"I will transmit them now," she said, somehow managing to make the statement suggestive.

Kane watched as the readout flashed on his computer screen. "Readout accepted," he said.

"Are we even?" asked Ardala, injecting a pathetic

note into her voice.

Kane cocked an eyebrow. "Are we ever?" he asked. "Would you want to be?"

Her lips drew together smugly. "I like exacting payment," she said.

"And paying?"

"Sometimes."

Kane chuckled once more.

"I always pay my debts," she said righteously. "It makes for much more pleasant relations."

Kane smiled at her. His strikingly handsome face was as irresistible to her as her sensuous appeal was to him. She returned his smile, glad she had managed to preserve their partnership. Kane was a useful friend and a wicked enemy. All things considered, she preferred the former.

"There is another matter," said Kane.

"Oh?" she asked.

Kane nodded. "Loose ends."

"Your men?"

"Yes." Poxon and Malone knew too much. Had the raid on Mercury been successful, they would have shared in the profit, over and above their fees. Without that extra cash, Kane did not trust their mouths.

"Remove them," suggested Ardala.

"No. They are useful, and as reliable as any mercenary." His smile flashed. "I want an assignment for them in the belt until this blows over."

"That is no problem. I can always use security."

"Good. I'll send them out tonight."

"That's settled," said Ardala. "Anything else?"

"Only the pleasure of your company," said Kane.

"The pleasure is always mine," she replied.

The terminal screen went dark as Ardala ended the
transmission. If Kane had made her come to him, she
left him in her own time.

Kane terminated from his end, pleased with his
bargain. He had the plans for the laser, and he had a
good supply of crystals. His raid on the crystal farm
was an extra he did not share with Ardala. By the
time she discovered it, she would be in no position to
protest.

Kane considered the possibilities of having his own
superweapon, something capable of vast destruction
of a planet. It would make him master of the solar
system, for he had one advantage over RAM, NEO,
Mercury, and the other powers. He would use the
weapon. One man could live a sweet life on a well-
stocked space station. Civilization could not. He let
his fantasies run, dreaming of the concessions he
could demand. Ardala's easy acquiescence did not
concern him. It did not occur to him that someone
else might beat him to the pot of gold.

○   ○   ○   ○   ○

Dalton Gavilan sat at his desk, studying a small
leather-bound book. The pages were covered with a
clear hand, perfect row upon row of letters, flowing
from page to page. The book was his journal, begun at
a young age. It was his personal study of power, a useful chronicle that recorded the weakness of his adversaries. In it he recorded every incident, every piece of
information that might be of use in his climb to control of Mercury. As he got older, he included ideas and
projections for the moves he must make. His

thoughts were agitated, as agitated as the Mercurian political structure.

Logic told him that the time was not yet ripe for him to seize power, but the breaches in Mercurian security, and his father's growing absorption with the laser, worried him. He felt the power structure he had built his life around shivering under his feet. Yet he knew that to allow Gordon to develop his ideas, while building his own power block, was the intelligent course. When Gordon backed himself into a corner, his son could lay the blame for everything from taxes to food prices on his father's unfortunate shoulders. It would not do to sacrifice that advantage by acting too soon. He must wait.

Besides, there were other things to do besides wait for his father to take a bad step. He had to deal with his dear cousin Kemal. Dalton was irrationally afraid of Kemal's heritage. As the son of an eldest son, Kemal was naturally superior, a fact that rattled the depths of Dalton's heart. Dalton could not voice his feeling, could not even admit it to himself. Instead, he focused his own inadequacy in anger, anger that found a scapegoat in Kemal.

That Kemal professed no interest in ruling Mercury, Dalton did not believe. What other destiny was there for a Gavilan? He believed that Kemal's disinterest was a ploy to earn Gordon's trust. Had he the power, Dalton was sure that Kemal would have him executed as a menace to the state. This was exactly what Dalton intended to do.

But, to accomplish his purpose, he needed to build a case of treason around his cousin. He was beginning to pile the building blocks in place. He had begun by setting one of Gordon's paramours, Ramora, on him. Ramora was unaware of her position. She thought she was following Gordon's orders, as she had so often in the past.

Dalton smiled as he remembered her eagerness to please. He had handed her a note. "Father asked me to give you this," he said.

"Since when were you Gordon's errand boy?" she had asked saucily, reaching for the note.

"He would trust no other messenger," Dalton had said. "He bade me to stress the importance of your mission, and its utter secrecy. You are not even to speak of it to him. As you can see—" Dalton had indicated the note with a brown finger—"you are to report to me." The ruse had been easy, and the memory was sweet.

Dalton had conceived the idea months before, but it had taken time to implement. As Gordon, he instructed Ramora to write any intelligence she got from Kemal down and stuff it into the antique vase in Gordon's study—a location to which any family member had easy access. So far, the ploy had worked.

Although Kemal was not succumbing to her attempts at seduction, he had been made to notice her. Dalton decided the time had come to change his tactics. He scrabbled in his lower desk drawer for the thick white paper and envelopes he had filched from his father's desk. He dug into the drawer, for he had made sure they were not easily found. In the middle of a stack of his personal security files, a few sheets of paper sat. Holding the files back, he grabbed the edge of the paper and pulled.

The whole batch of files flipped, cascading onto the

floor. Dalton snarled a curse and bent to pick them up before they became further disarranged. He shuffled the files into a semblance of order and shoved them back into the drawer next to a plain steel box with a key lock, then slammed the door shut. He placed the paper before him on the desk and got out a fountain pen that was a duplicate of Gordon's.

He pursed his lips and wondered how to proceed. Kemal was not being swayed by Ramora's charms. Perhaps he could be swayed by pity.

"Little bird," he wrote, using Gordon's pet name for her. "It is time to try another approach. If you cannot share his bed, become his friend. Tap the waters of his pity. You are a plaything of a rich man, not a person . . ."

Dalton continued writing industriously, forging his father's handwriting as he had so often as a child, when he wished to evade the wrath of his tutors.

Chapter Twenty-nine

Duernie crept through Mercury Prime's duct
work. Duernie was intimately acquainted
with the station's ventilation system. Not so
long before, she and Kemal Gavilan had taken a similar route, trying to escape from the station. Now she
was reversing the process. She was looking for one of
the computer cable tubes. If she could find a major
link, she could use the maintenance terminal to access the computer system.

She crawled carefully, for the duct was slick. If she
were to slip, the sound would be audible for a hundred yards. The duct was also hot, which told Duernie that she was still close to the loading docks. The

Gavilans reserved comfort for their own apartments, and they were not overly concerned with those who served them.

She followed the twists and turns patiently, glad to be free of the gossamer bales. They had been a flimsy camouflage, dangerous and insecure. She had been at the mercy of the dockhands who were handling the lot. She felt much better as master of her own actions.

Here and there a vent sent shafts of light from the hallways into the tube. The reflections on the shiny surface were disorienting, but Duernie had learned the trick of dealing with them. She focused on each grate where the light blazed, clinging to it until she reached the opening, then searched ahead for the next one. She passed twelve of them before she found a cable tube.

Sweat was pouring down her face. She pulled a kerchief out of her pocket, twisted it, and tied the orange band around her head.

The tube was located ten feet from the nearest vent. She crawled carefully to the vent and peered through the grating. It opened onto a hallway that branched in two directions. Such junctions contained service closets. The cable tube ran into one. She knew the closet would contain a computer tie-in and viewscreen, used for testing cable.

She popped the vent cover, trying to make as little noise as possible, and slid it inside the duct. The corridor was empty, but she cocked her head, listened for approaching footsteps, then slipped out of the vent and vaulted lightly to the floor. Sure enough, there was a service closet, marked with a stylized circuit juncture, ten feet away. She hurried to it, hit the door

release, and was safely inside. The door closed after
her. Duernie turned on the lights.

At the back of the closet was the computer block
and a small terminal screen. She went to the terminal, took a deep breath, and hit the activator button.
The screen zapped to life. Across the bottom of the
screen ran a priority message in red.

At first she ignored it, trying to find the station's
floor plan, but when she caught the word "Mariposa"
in the transmission, she read it carefully. The message contained notification of Gordon Gavilan's reac-
tivation of the chaff devices on the satellites, and the
information that all access to the Mariposas was now
under priority security. The computer security was
expanded into layers of blocks and traps so that anyone without the right codes would find his access
point burned out. Physical security had been increased as well. There were now armed guards, both
outside and inside the Mariposa power station on
Mercury Prime, that computer system that allocated
the distribution of the Mariposas' power. All personnel associated with it were now required to have
security-one clearance.

Duernie's heart sank. No deception would get her
through that blockade. She found the audio line on
the computer terminal and cut it in, turning the volume down so that it was barely audible.

"Station forty-one. We have run a sweep. All clear."

"Station six. Nothing in this sector."

"Station fourteen. We are clean."

She stared into the computer screen, patches of
sweat under her arms and down her back, and cursed
with a concentration that would have made a spacer

blush. She rebelled against the uselessness she felt. Every move she made was wrong. When she tried to accomplish something, she ended by despoiling it. She had been the voice of the Dancers with Kemal, hoping to make a Gavilan understand the lives and feelings of those who mined the desert so that the Sun Kings might have gold cutlery. She tried to give him a different perspective, an understanding of the hard life on Mercury's surface. She ended by leading her people down a path of destruction, straight into the teeth of the Gavilan machine.

She blamed herself for Kemal's actions. She should have known she could not trust a Gavilan, no matter how personable he seemed, no matter how kind he claimed to be. She should never have trusted him, should have kept her guard up. Instead, she had succumbed to his charms, falling in love with a man without a conscience.

"Weakling!" she snarled viciously at herself. "Contemptible, spineless woman! Have you a brain and a backbone?" she asked. "I do not think so. I think you gave those away when you gave your heart."

She stopped, her rock-hard silence a resolve as tough as granite.

"I will never give my heart again," she whispered. "Not to any living thing that can turn it against me. I will be strong! Strong!"

Her habitual frown deepened. Her angular face lost its attraction under the stress of her emotions. It was drained of femininity, of warmth. She stifled any flicker of pity or hint of desire. In their absence, another emotion took root, growing like wildfire in the fertile soil of her desecrated heart. She resolved to exact payment for her pain—and for the pain of her people. She wanted revenge for the dishonor, for the loss, for the death of hope.

Kemal was within her grasp. He was on Mercury Prime, and, as a Gavilan, he would know the code to breach the Mariposas' security. All she had to do was discover his exact location, then make her way to him without being caught.

"Sector six-five," said the computer terminal as the different sections of the space station continued to check in on the routine security sweep. "Loading docks are clean, though a dockhand thought he saw someone among the latest shipment of gossamer."

"Acknowledged," replied the security chief. "Keep your eyes open."

Duernie's heart thudded. The security squad was close to her hiding place. She had to get out. She found the floor plans she had been seeking earlier and began to scan them for Kemal's quarters. Level after level of the station flashed by, as much of a warren as anything beneath Mercury's surface. She was beginning to despair when the family level appeared. The Gavilans had an entire level of the space station for their personal use. It was coded and scrambled, and it took several minutes for Duernie to identify the different suites.

She found Kemal's rooms. There was only one recorded entrance, making the suite a dead end. She smiled at the analogy, thinking how apropos she intended to make it. Her photographic memory recorded the location, and she slipped out of the closet. The corridor was still empty, but she could hear footsteps. She leaped to the vent, grasped the sides with her strong brown fingers, and pulled herself up, her body sliding into the opening as the security squad rounded the corner. She froze, just inside the opening, holding her breath. The missing grate, if it were noticed, was a dead giveaway. She prayed that the squad would not look up.

Her prayers were answered. The drudgery of their routine had made the men careless, and they merely opened the door to the maintenance closet, peeked in, and continued on their way.

Duernie relaxed in relief, then carefully replaced the vent cover. The wire framework made her feel illogically secure. Her thoughts returned to Kemal.

Kemal Gavilan would not pay under any court system on Mercury for the wrong he had done her people or the humiliation he had heaped upon her. If he were to be brought to justice, it would be by her hand. Duernie extracted a knife from the sheath on her leg. Its wide blade glittered, even in the diffused light of the duct. She ran a finger along its cutting edge, testing it.

The blade's glitter was hypnotizing, full of rainbows and refracted light. She found it beautiful. It was a symbol of the justice she craved. With it a man might be cut down to size. He would no longer be a member of a privileged group. He would be a man begging for life, and he would be begging it of her.

Chapter Thirty

Really, my dear, you shouldn't pout. It ill becomes you."

Hauptman Raug's voice was smug. As the host of Russo-American Mercantile's gala reception, he would be at the head of the receiving line. Putting Ardala out of humor was next to impossible, for she always got her own way. To see her at a disadvantage was a satisfaction he had not expected. She had caused him some annoyance in the past, and he was quick to seize the opportunity, however small, for revenge.

He glanced appreciatively at her tall figure. Her hair was pulled back in a roll running up the back of her head. A jet-colored ornament shaped like a fan sparkled on either side of it. She wore a sheath of fine black net covered with jet beads. They sparkled intoxicatingly as she moved, darkening where the contours of her body condensed them, lightening under the strain of a curve. The dress had a high collar that set off her long neck and served to emphasize the dramatic "V" down her front. She moved with the sinuous grace of a cat, her head high, but anger flickered in her eyes.

"I am not pouting," Ardala finally returned. "You know how I feel about last-minute invitations."

"Then why did you come?" asked Raug.

Ardala snorted. "Business."

Raug's slick smile flashed. "It is comforting to know you are totally motivated by greed."

"Not totally," said Ardala, lowering her eyelids so that her long black lashes swept her cheeks.

"Your pardon. How could I forget the pulse of hormones in your blood?"

"You are bitter, Raug," she said silkily. Ardala's full lips drew up at the corners. The thought gave her pleasure.

"For once," Raug said severely, "I want you to behave yourself. I don't care what you do once the reception is over, but try to remember that you are here to lend support to RAM's cause."

"It's all such a bore," she said, turning away from him to stare out the window of his private limousine.

The Martian countryside, perfect in its landscaping, a park of manicured beauty, slipped by the windows. They rose slowly through the Martian atmosphere, and the patterns of planting and city

were more apparent. They were a geometric patch-
work that made a flawless quilt. Ardala watched it
idly as the limousine sailed toward Warhead's main
testing facility, a space station in tight orbit around
Mars.

As they neared the station, they passed other pleasure craft, all headed in the same direction. Ardala
recognized several of the ships. The reception would
include the highest members of the Martian court.
One of her eyebrows quirked appreciatively, and she
began to calculate ways to turn the event to her
advantage.

The limousine whined to a halt, and they waited
impatiently for docking coordinates. Finally, the ship
surged forward and powered down into a military
slip. When the docking tube was in place, Ardala rose
majestically. Raug smiled at her. "Figured an angle,
my dear?" he asked.

"If you wish me to act as your escort instead of the
other way around, you'd better get on your feet," she
said.

Raug rose obligingly and offered the imperious
beauty his arm. "Permit me, my dear."

"I'd not choose to," she said, accepting his arm.
"Perhaps another time."

Raug shook his head, wondering if she could take a
breath without consciously trying to seduce every
man she saw. Of course, with most men, seduction
took no effort. They fell at her feet in an abject slavery of passion. He knew she enjoyed fencing with a
man she could not deceive. He had known her since
birth, and he knew there were few men who were a
match for her. He knew she felt nothing but contempt

for most men, considering them weaklings to play with, and he knew she had no real affection for him. She did, however, acknowledge a grudging respect for a man who was as deceitful and greedy as she was, and made no bones about it.

They left the ship, moving slowly down the tube. As they entered Warhead's lobby, Raug begged leave.

"I must go and be official, my dear. No doubt, you can amuse yourself."

"No doubt," replied Ardala, dismissing him before he had a chance to leave. She sailed through the throng, accepting a glass of white wine from the first harried waiter who passed.

The invitation to this reception had been unexpected. Ardala's profession as an information broker kept her apprised of most major military projects, but she had heard nothing of new developments from Warhead since their production of the ill-fated Krait fighter.

The far end of the lobby was completely covered by a white curtain. It ran three stories high. Ardala knew it covered a wall of transparent plasti. Warhead was in the habit of parking its newest achievements behind the window, so that prospective buyers would be dazzled by the engineering technology at first glance.

"I haven't heard anything about a major new discovery," said a man beside her. "Have you?"

"No." There was a cold note in the word.

"Why, Ardala! As lovely as always. We don't see enough of you, my dear."

"That is because I choose not to be bored," Ardala answered, turning to the source of the voice.

Her aunt Eustancia fluttered before her. Short for a Martian, she was still a pretty woman, though past middle age. She lacked the imperious nature so common in the Valmar family. This especially annoyed Ardala, since her aunt was a notch closer to the throne. Ardala was pleased to see that her words had flustered her aunt.

"Really, child! Will you never learn manners?"

"Never," said Ardala firmly.

Raug, a few feet away, repressed a smile at the thought that anyone could call Ardala "child." She had been a dangerous woman at two years old.

"Nevertheless, you must visit us sometime. Your uncle Alvin would be so happy to see you." Eustancia's nervous hands described her feelings.

Ardala found her aunt's effusiveness distasteful. She smiled wickedly, and her voice went to the low register, full of honey. "I know he would," she said. "He has always been a favorite uncle," she said. "We seem to . . . connect."

Ardala played dirty games.

"Um. Well," said Eustancia helplessly. "I must fly—they're about to start the presentation."

"Yes," returned Ardala. "Do that." She turned away royally, dismissing Eustancia as she would a slave.

"Welcome." Raug's official voice cut into the conversation. "Welcome to Warhead. I would like to present the new president of the company, Joachim Parsonawitz."

A tall man, even for a Martian, Parsonawitz ascended the makeshift dais humbly. Ardala applauded his performance. It suited a new president on the occasion of his first major presentation.

"Once again, welcome," said Joachim. "Welcome to the most stupendous creation of the century. You are a privileged few, my friends. You will see, for the first time, a power mankind had dreamed of for all the years of his evolution."

There were scattered bursts of applause from the carefully planted company screamers.

"I come before you a humble man. I never dreamed, when I accepted the position of president of the largest munitions firm on Mars, that I would have the honor of presenting such a find to you." He lowered his head modestly.

Ardala ignored him. Her gaze was on the curtains, and her eyes had narrowed to black slits.

"Once in a great while, we make a discovery that can change the course of history. I tell you today, this discovery will define history!"

Again there was a burst of applause.

"RAM has suffered an ignominious rebellion at the hands of a few renegade upstarts from a ravaged planet. In the end, it was not cost-effective to continue the conflict. Nothing would have been gained. Earth is no longer a major asset. We left her barren, wasted, but the insult remains. It burns at the depths of every Martian soul."

Ardala's black eyes darted to Parsonawitz's face. Her mouth hardened.

"We will not, in the end, tolerate that insult. In the end, Earth will bow to our power, for we hold the reins to the one thing it cannot exist without: money."

Ardala's mouth pursed with tension.

"Power is the final answer. He who commands it commands the system. That privilege has always been the prerogative of Mars. Until now."

The tension was not exclusive to Ardala. Parsonawitz was touching on a sore subject, one every Martian would have liked to forget. His reception included those most intimately associated with the defeat.

"I tell you that Warhead is prepared to give Mars back that power. We have in our hands the means."

There was a gasp of appreciation from one of his supporters.

"Yes," said Parsonawitz, bouncing off the arranged reaction. "I am not joking. Once more, Mars will take her rightful place as the emperor of the solar system. You—" and he pointed dramatically at the gathering—"are here to determine which individuals will own that power. This is an auction, ladies and gentlemen. What am I bid for the ability to rule a region? What am I bid?"

Coinciding with his final words, the white curtain drew back. Floating between the two dry dock arms was a huge laser, its lens a mass of Sun Flower crystals. Beside it, Gordon's prototype would look like a toy.

"Ladies and gentlemen, I present to you the Warhead Laser XIV, capable of slicing a region to rubble with the awesome power of our own star. What am I bid?"

Those in the room stood in stunned silence. Only Ardala moved. With a growl like a cornered cat, she whirled and stalked through the crowd. Her movement brought the others to life. They made way for her, parting in front of her anger like torn cloth.

Ardala was furious. She knew she had to get away from the company, or she'd kill Parsonawitz with her bare hands. She was so angry, she did not even consider colorful ways for him to die. She merely wanted him dead. He had stolen what was hers and was parading it in front of her. She should have been the one to reap millions from the laser. The plans were hers! She had gone to infinite trouble to secure and protect the specifications for it. She whirled out of the lobby in a cloud of anger so black that the guards at the door drew back from her as if she carried a plague.

Chapter Thirty-one

Kane lunged. His superbly balanced body was an extension of his weapon. He held a plain dagger in his right hand, its old-fashioned blade a fraction duller than the mono knife's. His sparring partner brandished a similar weapon. The two circled warily.

The sight of Kane stripped to the waist would have made a sculptor cry. He was in perfect condition, armor plates of muscle without the showy bulk so popular in fiction. He was a trifle sinewy, a trifle spare, but he was lightning fast. His naked torso carried few scars, which was significant. He fought with a light in his eyes and a smile on his face.

The same could not be said of his opponent. He was a professional, a gladiator from Venus. Before his employment as Kane's personal opponent, he had fought for pay in the arenas of Mars. For him, combat was not pleasure. It was a job from which he must emerge victorious. As a sparring partner, he knew his place. He must give his employer a good fight, but he must never win. If it looked as if he might, he must make a mistake.

Kane was entirely cognizant of the gladiator's philosophy. He applauded it, for he knew that, should the competition become heated, he would lose perspective. He would fight to win, and for Kane, winning meant living while another man died. He had not been trained in an arena where sportsmanship and referees kept the conflict civil. He had received his education on the streets of Old Earth, in one of the toughest arcologies extant. He had learned early to accept no quarter. The enemy you leave alive will return to haunt you. In light of his temperament, he was glad of his opponent's approach. It saved him having to find another, possibly less accomplished, partner.

He grunted as the gladiator, with his greater size and longer reach, made him duck and jump to one side. He moved like a cat, in an acrobatic leap that placed him beyond his adversary's weapon yet ready to face him. His opponent, for all his size, was quick and crafty. He had not survived arena fighting for ten years without learning some things. He countered Kane's move, landing in front of him, and they circled once more.

The two combatants occupied the game room in

Kane's stronghold on Luna. This was a daily workout
for the mercenary, though he varied the routine with
unarmed combat. It was part of his regimen to keep
himself in top condition. Kane knew he was the best
man in the system, but he wanted to make sure others knew it as well.

Sweat shone on his skin, showing off his rippling
muscles as if they had been rubbed with oil. The slick
feeling of clean sweat was like oil, lubricating his
actions, making him a marvel of movement. He
switched the knife to his other hand, just for practice.

His opponent was quick to take advantage, but
Kane was quicksilver, sliding out of his grasp. The
knife missed, slicing air.

At the back of his mind Kane heard the game room
door open. He did not miss a step or a slash as one of
his servants approached. "What is it?" he said pleasantly, making a wicked stab toward the gladiator.

"There is a call for you from Warhead, sir. It is
Parsonawitz."

"The new director." Kane nodded as he leaped
backward, twisting to avoid the blade. "Tell him I
will be with him momentarily."

The servant departed, and Kane turned his full attention to his partner. "It seems I must end the competition," he said.

The gladiator met his blade, and the two weapons
clashed as they locked at the hilts, each man testing
the other's strength. The gladiator grimaced as he
bore down on his smaller opponent. Kane did not
give.

The gladiator backed off, and so did Kane. The two
faced each other with questions in their eyes, then

lowered their weapons. Kane chuckled. "Good match," he said, slapping his sparring partner on the arm. "Tomorrow."

The man nodded, breathing heavily. He was not as young as Kane, and his heavier body required more effort to move.

Kane sheathed his knife and picked up a towel. He did not bother to put on a shirt as he headed for his office. He wiped the sweat from his face on the way, then slung the towel around his neck. When he arrived at the office, Parsonawitz's solemn countenance was regarding him mournfully from the viewscreen.

"You take your time, for a hired gun," said Warhead's new administrator.

"Careful," said Kane, his smile deceptive. "I may not choose to work for you."

It was plain that Parsonawitz had not met a man of Kane's stripe before. "When I can offer you so much money that you won't have to work for a year?" he asked.

"Regardless of the amount of money you have to offer. If I do not like a job—or the man offering it—I will decline. I do not need the work, and you do need me. I presume that is why you called."

Annoyance flickered across Parsonawitz's face, but he suppressed it immediately, realizing that he would have to take another tack with his company's most exclusive security man. Belatedly, he remembered Kane's past. He was not dealing with a malleable colonial. Kane was Earth born and NEO trained. Although he had forsaken his past, he could not forsake the core of stubborn independence that made him not only the best mercenary in the system but the most difficult.

"I have a job for you."

"I am honored," said Kane sardonically.

"There is a good deal of money involved."

"How much?" Kane was flippant.

Parsonawitz named a formidable sum.

Kane smirked. He knew his expression would infuriate the executive, but he held the cards. He had built a fortune, which meant he worked as he wished. His clients came to him, thinking it a favor if he deigned to work for them.

"You seem unimpressed," said Parsonawitz tightly.

"Add another hundred thousand credits," said Kane, "and I might be willing to listen."

Parsonawitz frowned. "I do not have to deal with you, Kane."

"No. But I am worth my price."

"The last time you worked for Warhead, you did not fulfill your contract," he said nastily, referring to Kane's abortive attempt to deliver experimental fighters during the inception of the Martian Wars.

"Your entire board reviewed that incident," said Kane. "They found the circumstances extenuating."

"Are you free or not?" asked Parsonawitz brusquely.

"I am free. What do you want me to do?"

Parsonawitz hit a button, and the screen behind him changed, showing a huge apparatus floating between two arms of a dry dock bay. "That is our newest achievement," he said.

Kane recognized the laser immediately. No wonder, he thought, Ardala had been so willing to give him the plans, when she had already sold them to RAM.

"It is a solar-powered laser, capable of massive impact. We intend to test it in the asteroid belt."

"A mining laser? You're a munitions corporation."

"We will test on rock," said Parsonawitz shortly.

Kane repressed a smile. "What do you want of me?"

"We want you to handle transportation and security for the lens during testing. We have a handful of specialists involved in this project. We need all of them to test it. Therefore, I am contracting security."

Kane nodded. He did not want to let Parsonawitz know his attitude had changed. He wanted access to RAM's new toy in the worst way. "As I said, make it worth my while."

"Seven hundred thousand credits," snapped Parsonawitz, "and a bonus of three hundred more when the tests are completed and the laser is returned to our headquarters."

"That's more like it."

"You'll do it then?"

Kane let Parsonawitz stew while he examined the giant version of the laser. It was an awesome achievement, a doomsday weapon. With it a man would be able to rule the system. He wanted it as badly as he had ever wanted anything.

"Take the ceiling off my expenses, and I'll accept the job."

Parsonawitz's eyes crackled with anger. "What guarantee do I have that you will handle such an expense account judiciously?" he asked, doing his best to insult Kane without losing him.

"None," replied the mercenary sweetly. "It boils

down to this: you want me or you don't. Suit yourself."

Parsonawitz glared at him. He would have died before letting Kane know his board had instructed him to get Kane for security at all costs. "Very well," he said coldly. "I will meet your demands."

Kane nodded. "And I will nursemaid your pet project," he returned.

"You will collect the laser three days from now. It is due in the belt in a week. You must be on time, or we will lose millions. Do you understand?"

"Perfectly," replied Kane.

Parsonawitz studied him. Kane's handsome face was a mask of innocent interest, his eyes as honest as a green summer sea. Parsonawitz knew he could not trust what he saw. "You will be given an advance of one-third."

"One-half," said Kane.

"I do not have the time to haggle with a paid watchdog!" Parsonawitz could no longer control his anger, and Kane smiled, pleased at having managed to make him lose his temper.

"Then give me what I ask," said Kane.

"All right. One-half. The rest upon completion of the tests."

"Done," said Kane. He picked up the towel and lazily rubbed his arm with it, dismissing the mogul.

"Kane." Parsonawitz demanded his attention.

"Yes?"

"See that you do not disappoint me. As you have seen, I have little patience. I do have a lot of influence. If you do not keep your bargain, I will see you in irons."

Kane was not impressed by the threat. Daggers of challenge flashed through the deceptive depths of his green eyes. "That has been tried before. As you can see, I am quite free."

"Now, I grant," said Parsonawitz. "Do not underestimate me."

Kane smiled again. "I do not intend to make that mistake again. I assure you, sir, your profile is thoroughly outlined in my personal security files. I know exactly what I am dealing with. Do you?"

Parsonawitz's eyes hardened. "See that you are there on time," he said, and cut the transmission.

Kane rubbed the back of his neck with the towel. It felt good against the cool wetness of drying perspiration. He felt like a child with a sack of candy. He had played an abortive part in Ardala's operation on Mercury, but he had come out of it with a bonus she did not know about and the plans for the laser. Now he was being asked to shepherd an existing laser to the asteroid belt. RAM was making conquest so easy. The reins of state were falling into his hands as if the gods decreed his superiority.

He blessed the Martian conglomerate for doing his work for him. RAM had saved him the time, trouble, and expense of constructing the laser. From what he had been able to see, it had done a superb job of it. Now the company proposed to test it for him, saving him that step as well.

He rubbed the towel across his wet hair until it stood up in dark tufts. He was facing the greatest opportunity of his life. With the laser as his army, he could order the solar system, returning control to genetically pure humans, not the bastard strains of genetic manipulation. The Martians called themselves superior, a master race. To Kane, they were freaks and not of nature. Their bodies were genetically adapted to Mars through human interference. They were not worthy to govern, for they had not been tried by the forces of the universe.

He ached for power. He ached to show every man who had ever slighted or bested him that they were the losers, not he. He wanted to force worlds to come to him, as he had just forced Parsonawitz. Let them grovel at his feet. He thought of Ardala, and his eyes warmed. One of the greatest pleasures he would have would be to make her beg him for mercy, for life, and for love. He would make her fawn at his feet like a lapdog, or lose her life. He knew Ardala. He knew she would do it, plotting all the while for the day when she could wreak revenge.

"Into my hands," he said softly to himself. "Into my hands they have commended their spirits."

The laser was his. He had known it from the moment Ardala told him of its existence. Now, even the fates bowed to the knowledge, giving him the means to rule.

Chapter Thirty-two

Kemal carefully coded the final set of blocks into his computer. It had taken him two hours to find and isolate all of his uncle's bugs. The Mercury Prime computer system was Gordon's personal spy network, aimed at keeping track of key personnel. He had found sixty-eight independent blocks, set to monitor his personal communications and his rooms. He hoped he had them all. To miss even one would mean his life.

Moreover, he could not allow Gordon's computer eyes to realize that they were no longer watching him. He had arranged careful electronic simulations for them to monitor, and prayed the ruse would work.

He had to contact Huer.dos, and the only avenue he
had was the Mercury Prime communications link. Of
course, it would be much more secure to contact his
friend in NEO from a space-borne ship, but explain-
ing to Gordon, and especially to Dalton, why he
wanted to take a pleasure cruise would have been
even more difficult than the job he had just
completed.

With the recent setbacks, Gordon was sensitive
about anything that could not be explained at least
six different ways, and Kemal knew Dalton was perennially suspicious of him.

Kemal flexed his fingers, hoping his calculations
were accurate. If they were, one coded cross-link
would put him on the NEO emergency channel and
in direct contact with Huer. He punched the numbers
into his console and waited, not knowing whether
they would bring him the voice of a friend or his own
death.

It took a few minutes for the link to be completed.
Kemal lived ten years during those moments. Finally the link beeped. "The line is open," it said in a
mechanical voice.

"This is Switch Hitter," said Kemal, borrowing his
friend Buck's ancient baseball allusion. He knew the
references would immediately attract Huer's attention. "Shortstop, acknowledge. Strike three."

"Kemal!" Huer's voice was full of relief. His image
popped onto the small screen, precise, slim, with concerned brown eyes. "We got your present," he said.

"Thank the lucky stars," said Kemal.

Kemal sagged with relief. "I wondered. Then NEO
has complete readouts on the laser, and by now, the

plans for a larger model."

"Yes," answered Huer. "But we've heard nothing but rumors. Something about a strike on Mercury. Was that you?"

"Yes and no," replied Kemal.

"Barney dragged the laser into Salvation as if it were a piece of trash. It's tied up there now, in plain sight."

Kemal grinned.

"What about Gordon's giant model?"

"Destroyed. I am afraid I set Ardala up to do my dirty work for me."

Huer whistled. "You may have more to reckon with than Ardala—though, I admit, that's enough. Rumor has it Killer Kane made that strike on Mercury."

"Kane. I'm sorry to have him for an enemy."

"For a young man, you sometimes show flashes of intelligence," remarked Huer.

"He's nothing to joke about," said Kemal soberly. "I've seen him in action."

"And Ardala?"

"She scares me," Kemal admitted. "I know there's no limit to her capacity for revenge. I think I may have to try to get out of that one."

"She is a woman of strong passions."

"More than that," said Kemal. "I have never before met anyone I could honestly say was evil. Ardala is. There is not one shred of human feeling in her."

"I don't think, from your reactions, that you know of the latest developments."

Kemal shook his head. What are you talking about?" he asked.

Huer sighed. "I really hate to tell you this after I

bullied you into taking on your whole family. RAM has somehow gotten the plans for the laser. It has managed to construct a model even larger than the one Gordon proposed. It is awaiting testing now."

"You mean I risked my neck for nothing?" Kemal's earnest face was dismayed.

"It looks that way," said Huer.

"Wonderful. Huer, I want out. I am playing this game too close to the edge. My life is in danger from more than one source. I know my family, with the possible exception of my cousin Tix, wants me dead. The Dancers think I betrayed them, and I am sure they want me dead. One Dancer in particular bears me a grudge. I am not a popular man. I would like to remain a live one."

"Kemal, you have established a wonderful cover. Gordon will not give up. I have studied him. This setback will serve to strengthen his resolve. In spite of RAM's weapon, he will not rest until he has his own. Once Gordon Gavilan fixes on an idea, he is a bulldog."

"And you want me to watch him and report my family's actions to NEO."

Huer looked surprised at Kemal's tone. "Yes. Is that a problem?"

"They are my family. Despite the fact there is no love lost between us, I do not like spying on them. Why can't NEO let Mercury handle its own affairs?"

"Oh, we would like to," replied Huer, "but inventions like the laser affect us all."

"The Mercurian laser is gone. I want out."

"Then you'll have to escape on your own. I don't have the resources to buck the Gavilans."

"And NEO? Will my reputation with NEO be intact?"

"When you are free, I will see to it," promised Huer.

"I have accomplished nothing," said Kemal sadly, "except the deaths of the technicians with the laser."

"That is not true. You have prevented an unstable man from wielding power he cannot understand."

"But if RAM has a laser—"

"RAM is not as immediately unstable as your uncle. Besides, RAM rules by committee and board. Its decisions are rarely whimsical. By the time the lens is ready for deployment, we will have an operation planned to destroy it. Do not worry about the RAM model."

"If, as you say, Gordon will attempt to build another laser, then what good did it do to destroy the first one?"

"It bought time," said Huer. "Time for things to happen. You have accomplished more than you realize. You have made it possible to think, not just react. NEO has little strength for action that is not necessary."

"I've done what you asked, and now I'm going to find a way out of here," said Kemal. "But I need to have you within call. If I can break free of Mercury's sphere of influence, I'll need your protection—and I would not mind having some warning of the headhunters out to scalp me."

"You'll have it," said Huer.

"Promise me you will tell Buck of my activities," said Kemal tightly. "At least he should know. If anything happens—if I don't make it out—I don't want my name sullied. I don't want to be known as a traitor to my friends."

Huer's voice became gentle. "I will do as you ask," he said.

"I can't keep the transmission on too long," said Kemal, "or Gordon's communication techs will get suspicious. I'm signing off."

"Take care, Kemal. You are a part of us," said Huer.

A lump rose in Kemal's throat as Huer's image faded from the screen. It had been too long since he had been with those who cared for him, and now it was a computer-generated personality who touched him. The irony was cutting. He loosed Gordon's computer blocks, rose from the console, and ran his fingers through his hair. He crossed to the bed and sank down on it, kicking off his boots. He was drained.

Kemal stretched out and switched off all light but a soft lamp over his door. He closed his tired eyes and rubbed them. They itched like fury, and he knew the one remedy for them was sleep. He concentrated on relaxing, and soon he was snoring lightly. The sound reverberated in the room, a gently rhythmic rumble.

The minutes ticked by, and Kemal's snores rose in volume as his slumber deepened. He thrashed once, then lay still.

In a corner of the room, a ventilation duct filtered the air. It was a yard wide and half a yard high. The duct covering made a squeak of protest as it was pushed from the wall. A pair of slim brown hands caught it as it loosened, preventing it from falling. The cover was pulled back into the duct, and a head appeared in the opening.

The room was dim enough that the figure was no more than a black silhouette. The head turned toward Kemal, who slept peacefully. It studied him for a long time. Finally the figure grasped the edge of the opening and pulled itself forward. Nimbly the slim body slithered out of the opening, clinging to the sides of the hole. Without a sound, it dropped to the floor in a crouch.

For a long moment, it stayed there, not moving, not breathing, then it slowly rose. The figure stood erect, and even in the dim light, it was apparent that it was a woman. The formfitting garment suited her lanky frame. In one swift move, she stooped and pulled a slim knife from a sheath inside her boot. The blade caught the light in a white curve, deadly, blinding.

Step by cautious step she advanced on Kemal. He mumbled in his sleep but did not move. She reached the edge of the bed and stood over him, the knife in one hand. She hesitated, momentarily undecided, and Kemal rolled over, flat on his back.

She was on him in a flash, her long legs locked around him as she straddled him, the knife pressed to his throat. In their swiftness and violence, her movements were practiced.

Kemal reacted immediately. His military training saved his life. He gave one jerk, then lay still, the knife his only reality. He knew a deep breath might kill him.

"Don't move," said Duernie. "I want you to know who it is who kills you."

Kemal lay like one already dead.

"You used me. Like all men, you used me for your own ends. To be betrayed by the heart—that is pain, but to be used to betray one's friends, one's family—that is the death of honor."

Kemal started to open his mouth, but Duernie pressed the knife against his neck, and he subsided.

"You are worse than the others. I can live without my heart. I have done it for years. I cannot live without honor."

"Let me speak!" Kemal croaked, moving as little as possible.

"Why not?" said Duernie. "It will do you no good."

"I did not betray you."

"Liar!" said Duernie.

"I could not betray a friend. I had to prevent my uncle from killing us all."

"You would say anything to live," she said, her lip curling.

"No. Your respect means too much to me."

"I will prove it," she said. "Tell me you love me. If you do that, I will let you live."

Kemal closed his eyes. "I no longer know what I feel," he replied. "I only know you have been in my thoughts daily."

The answer was not what she expected.

Kemal felt the knife cold against the skin of his throat.

Chapter Thirty-three

Duernie's black eyes, as expressionless as stones, bored into Kemal's hazel ones. "Beg!" she said. "Beg for your life! Those are the only words I want to hear."

Kemal answered hotly. "Then I will say nothing, since you do not wish to hear the truth." The knife was a white glitter on his left.

"The truth! You do not know the meaning of the word." Her eyes were savage, her strong body hard against him.

"Duernie! I did not realize, when you led me to the crystal farm, what was happening. I was used, too, by my family and circumstances. Didn't I tell you to turn back?"

A flicker of doubt crossed Duernie's dark face, easing her frown.

"Duernie, I saved your life that day. It was the only reparation I could make at the time. I never meant to hurt the Dancers—or you. I have stayed on Mercury Prime to fight my uncle's paranoia." Kemal's face was as earnest as his argument.

"You wish to help the Dancers? Then give me the security code for computer access to the Mariposas, so I can destroy them. Trade me Gavilan wealth for Dancer revenge." Duernie's impassioned demand echoed the dark red flush of excitement on her high cheekbones.

Kemal thought fast. His life was in the balance, and he knew Duernie was a strong woman, as strong as the harsh surface of Mercury. She would not quail at exacting revenge. Her bronze face was inches from his, her wide brow reflecting the light, her black eyes catching it. He decided that if he wanted her to trust him, he would have to trust her. He swallowed, feeling the knife blade as he did so. "The code is 'chrysalis'," he said. "But if you would truly help your people, you will not use it."

"I will not listen to your lies!" she said. "I should kill you now."

Anger flashed in Kemal's gold-brown eyes. "Then why don't you?" he asked.

Duernie began to tremble, but her eyes were still hard.

"Duernie, you are my friend," said Kemal. "You saved my life. For this, circumstances have forced me to put you and your people in jeopardy. I am going to

trust you with the whole truth. I was responsible for
the destruction of Gordon's giant laser. And I betrayed Ardala. The laser she once owned is now in
NEO's hands, stolen from her by Black Barney." He
smiled ironically. "You are not the only one who
would like to kill me, if the truth were known. I have
remained on Mercury to try to circumvent my uncle's
military madness."

Duernie was trembling violently now, the knife
shaking in her hand. Kemal reached for it. Duernie's
hand ceased to tremble. "Why should I believe you?"
she asked.

"Because," said Kemal, "more than any woman I
have known, I respect you."

"Prove it!" she said, her coral mouth twisted with
the violence of her demand.

"All right, but you will have to let me up."

Duernie climbed off him, the knife under his left
ear.

Kemal moved slowly. He rose and went to the computer terminal, Duernie at his back. He sat down, accessed the station's power systems, then typed in the
word "chrysalis." "There," said Kemal. "Destroy
them. You will merely have damaged Gordon's
wealth. Or wait—help me—and we may accomplish
something for Mercury, and for the Dancers."

"How?" asked Duernie.

"I don't know," said Kemal honestly, "but it is the
reason I am still here. I would be wise to leave Mercury, but I am the one voice of freedom in the Gavilan
stronghold, though my family doesn't know it. Yet."

Duernie eyed the readout hungrily. She wanted to
destroy the Mariposas, but she wanted to believe Ke-

mal as well. Her heart and head battled for victory.

Suddenly the holographic eye on Kemal's terminal winked on. A tall man in royal robes materialized next to Kemal, a hand outstretched in warning.

Duernie jumped in surprise, and Kemal knew, in that moment, he might have disabled her. He also knew that to do so would kill all chances of regaining her trust. He remained where he was.

"Why do you threaten my son?" asked Ossip's computer-generated ghost.

"Your son?" Duernie looked from one to the other. The resemblance was indeed strong. Ossip had Kemal's clean features and slim frame, though he was taller than his son.

"I have alerted security," said the ghost. "You cannot escape."

"Father, she is my friend." Kemal spoke the truth of his heart.

Ossip reacted quickly. Like Huer, his eyes lost focus when he was accessing the computer. He turned to Kemal. "I have made the security alert a computer malfunction. Your friend holds a knife at your throat, Kemal."

"So she does," said Kemal ironically.

Duernie let the knife slide away from Kemal. "You did not have to say that."

"No," answered Kemal, "but it is true. You are my friend, even if I am no longer yours, and you are in deadly danger here on Mercury Prime."

"When I came here," said Duernie, her face drained, "I did not expect to escape, only to exact revenge. I have failed."

Kemal turned to Duernie and took her by the

shoulders. "The best revenge, Duernie, is to beat Gordon—and the system—at its own game, to secure the Dancers' position on Mercury, and our own as well. We must get you off Mercury Prime. How did you get here?"

"Cargo," Duernie replied succinctly, her severe mouth softened by a glint of humor.

"Then we will ship you back," he said with a grin, "but this time with a Gavilan label on the box. Can you get back to the hold?" asked Kemal.

"Yes." Duernie eyed the ventilator shaft.

"Is there one of those useful maintenance closets nearby?"

"Yes. I used it to cut into the computer," said Duernie.

"Meet me there in two hours." Kemal's hazel eyes danced. The plan that presented itself was definitely amusing. "And Duernie . . ."

"Yes?" she asked.

Kemal clasped her hand. "I will do everything in my power to protect Mercury—and the Dancers."

O O O O O

Two hours later, Duernie slipped from the uncomfortable, slippery confines of Mercury Prime's duct work, landing softly in the corridor. She was inside the maintenance closet in two strides.

Kemal was waiting for her, an imp of the devil sparkling in his eyes. He carried a spacesuit over one arm. It was brilliant yellow with red piping. Under the other arm was a matching helmet, its faceplate dark, polarized to help protect the wearer from the

Sun. He handed them to Duernie. "Ever fly a transport shuttle?" he asked.

She shook her head. "Just skimmers and jetcars."

"It's just a larger version."

"Where am I going?" she asked.

"Would Phidias Warren be suitable?" said Kemal.

Duernie's slim brown fingers froze on the suit's front closure. For the first time, her black eyes lost their haunted look.

Kemal nodded. "Get that suit on!" he said. "You're due to take off in ten minutes."

Duernie sealed the suit and reached for the helmet, but Kemal reached out and pulled her close. He kissed her firm coral lips gently, then released her, smiling. "Until we meet," he said, and handed her the helmet.

Without a word, Duernie placed the helmet over her head.

Kemal opened the door to the closet, peered down the corridor, and motioned for Duernie to follow him. They strode onto the loading dock. Kemal headed straight for a pile of crates. His cousin Tix was hovering over them protectively.

"Oh, K-Kemal!" Tix's excitement was obvious. His blue eyes shone. "I have n-never been so excited! When word c-came from Phidias Warren that they wanted to exhibit my sculpture, I was stunned! How d-did they know?"

"Word of talent flies fast," said Kemal evasively. The computer manipulations he had made to get Tix the exhibit had taken some fancy juggling and help from Ossip. Kemal patted a crate. "All success, Tix."

"Thank you." Tix watched fondly as two workers

hefted one of his masterpieces into the hold of a sturdy shuttle.

As the workers returned for the final box, Duernie moved casually toward the shuttle's open hold.

Tix caught her arm.

Duernie froze in her tracks, her heart pounding.

"Have a safe f-flight," said Tix, "and a soft landing. I hope the packing holds," he said fretfully.

"Your work will be fine. This is an experienced rocketjock," said Kemal, lying through his teeth. He disengaged Tix's hand, and Duernie disappeared into the ship.

Tix was watching the men secure the final box. They locked it to the hull with cables, then left the hold.

Kemal waved to Duernie, then gave her a thumbs-up signal. Duernie returned Kemal's gesture. The red warning light came on over the dock's doors, and the bay cleared.

From the safety of the control room, Tix and Kemal watched the shuttle warm up as the space doors began to open. The shuttle lifted slowly from the deck, its engines humming. Over his left shoulder, Kemal could hear the launch tech advising Duernie of her course. Duernie's monosyllabic answers, distorted on the communications link, sent a warm smile to Kemal's eyes. As the shuttle chugged slowly into space, he raised a hand once again in salute.

Tix took the gesture personally. "Thank you, K-Kemal. Without you, I would never have had the c-courage to take this opportunity."

Kemal's smile broadened. "Without you, Tix, there would have been no opportunity at all."

Kemal watched the shuttle move out of visual range. Duernie was on her way home, again an ally—the only one he had on Mercury. He was no longer alone.

THE INNER PLANETS TRILOGY

Book One:
FIRST POWER PLAY
John Miller

As the New Earth Organization rebuilds an Earth shattered by the Martian Wars, NEO sympathizer Kemal Gavilan receives a corpse and a cryptic message from the asteroids. The Mercurian prince sends master pirate Black Barney to find out what he can, but the answer is hot: they've uncovered a weapon that can focus the sun's energy for global annihilation! The Martian and Venusian powers insist they're innocent. Kemal is forced to rejoin the royal family he once rejected to learn the awful truth.

Book Three:
MATRIX CUBED
Britton Bloom

Kemal unravels instability in the Sun King empire and finds himself thrust into daunting circumstances. His problems are compounded by the fact that others—including RAM—may have developed remarkably similar laser projects. Available in May 1991.